Survive

The

Night

DERRYAN DERROUGH

DEDICATION

To my son, who takes his time with things, to make sure everything is as it's supposed to be. To my daughter, who flies by the seat of her pants, and figures it out later. To my wife, who takes care of me like I take care of her.

And to you, the reader. I hope you find something really cool to hold on to.

1

Clink.

Just a few short months ago, Dwight Durant did what he pleased. He was rich in money and allies.

Now, thanks to The Sound and Ivory Fox, Dwight thought about the next enemy around the corner. The prison was an ocean full of sharks. If he kept to himself and stayed out of trouble long enough, the parole board would surely reduce his sentence.

Sitting in his cell, he grimaced when he looked at his fingernails. He rubbed his thumb back and forth across the top of them, digging out the pockets of dirt settled underneath. His hair had grown back. He wasn't interested in a haircut, not in here. His sorry, soleless shoes lent little arch support. They were worthless to him. He was better off barefoot.

This cold, stale-smelling hellhole was Dwight's home for twenty-three hours a day, the remaining hour, for exercise. If he wanted to be out of his cell for longer than that hour, he had to earn it.

How the hell he got in this predicament in the first place kept him up, even as the lights shut off for the night.

Dwight rested his head on his bulky, misshapen pillow. The old mattress above his bunk sunk in with every movement from his cellmate.

"Nobody came to see you today?"

His counterpart's hollow, raspy voice broke Dwight out of his thoughtful haze. Dwight blinked long and hard. When he opened his eyes, he said, "Nope. Not today, Old-Timer."

"How many days is that?"

"As many days as I've been here, Old-Timer."

"Buchanan didn't come get you yet?"

Dwight snickered and shook his head. "I'm still here, right? And I'm gonna be here a while, too. Nobody answers when I call. Nobody's in a rush to visit. It's the same damn thing every day: I eat, sleep, and work out. Just trying to get through these days."

"Let me leave you alone, then."

The Old-Timer fell silent. Dwight closed his eyes.

"You scared?" the Old-Timer asked.

Dwight opened his eyes again. "Not for the reasons you think." He tightly clutched both lapels on his orange jumpsuit. "Look, I'm a few months into a five-year sentence. I can already feel the rot of jail on me. I should've just talked to Michael. I don't know what I was thinking. I should've never put that gun to Marissa's head."

"Who's Marissa, again?" the Old-Timer asked.

Dwight sighed. "Michael's daughter. She never did anything to me, and my dumb ass thought it'd be a great idea to hold up a restaurant at gunpoint. To be honest, I'm glad The Sound stopped me. I could've been in here 25 to life … like you."

The mattress above him moved when his cellmate laughed. "Don't say it like that! It ain't so bad in here once you get used to it. I heard The Sound is a *bad* boy. Just because we're holed up in this godforsaken place, don't mean the news don't circulate."

"Yeah. I know," Dwight drew out. He freed his lapels and looked at his wrist, opening and closing his fist. He winced. "My wrist still hasn't healed right."

"I hope time heals you, young man," the Old-Timer said. "I won't bother you no more. Get some rest."

"Yeah."

Dwight told anyone and everyone that The Sound stopped him. He struggled with the truth. The Sound merely slowed him down. The Ivory Fox stopped him in his tracks. The truth would bring more harassment than usual. If the truth got out, he'd be eaten alive.

The prison usually buzzed with chatter deep into the night. This night, it was eerily quiet. Dwight writhed around his bed, digging his back into the mattress. He tilted his head deeper into his pillow.

Just as Dwight closed his eyes, the sound of footsteps approaching opened them. The feet he heard smacked against the concrete corridor. Every cell in the building came alive with a mix of whispers and normal tones as the footsteps passed them. Dwight placed his hand on his chest. His heart raced. He sucked his bottom lip into his mouth and bit down.

The mattress above him moved again. A second later, the Old-Timer peered down at him, worry smeared across his face.

"What the hell is all that commotion?" he asked.

"Don't know," Dwight responded. "I'm sure it's nothing."

A prison guard stopped in front of their cell. Dwight avoided his gaze.

"You have a visitor," the guard said gruffly, then left.

Dwight's stomach dropped. Visitation never happened like this. He placed his hands on the edge of his bunk and pushed himself up. A silhouette slowly came to light.

"Michael?"

The anxiety washed off and a smile formed. He pushed off his bed and stood up. Michael placed his hand in the air. Dwight didn't take another step. Instead, he sat back down. His smile faded.

The guard re-appeared to push a chair inside the cell. Michael took a seat.

"So … here we are," he said.

Dwight couldn't help but show his excitement. "It's so good to see you." He threw a hand up to highlight his cell. "How do you like my new digs?"

Michael smirked. "Truthfully? Your living situation was better a few months ago."

"It's so good to see you, Michael," Dwight repeated. He wanted to get up and hug Michael, but stopped himself. He'd been waiting months for a visit. Of everyone Dwight knew, no one paid a visit, not even his parents. The surprise was more than welcome, but in the back of Dwight's mind, a nagging feeling of uneasiness set in.

"Let's be honest: You know why I'm here," Michael said.

The intensity in Michael's tone and eye contact only confirmed Dwight's reason for uneasiness. Dwight responded by sitting up straight.

"Look, Michael, I–"

Michael rapidly waved his hands in front of him. "No need to apologize. No need. Plus, I don't want to hear it."

Dwight nodded.

"Do me a favor. I need you to run something through my ears one time, just so I hear it from the horse's mouth."

"Sure," Dwight said.

"The night at the restaurant. Start to finish."

Dwight nodded. He felt the Old-Timer's eyes on him. Shaking it off, Dwight's attention returned to Michael.

Dwight said, "Okay, so … we went in the restaurant with money on our minds. We tri–"

Michael stood up. "I'm not listening to this nonsense."

Dwight took a deep breath and exhaled. "I'm sorry. I'll start over." He cleared his throat and said, "It was me and a few other guys. They had money on their mind. I had revenge on mine. I was just so mad, man."

"What were you mad about?" Michael asked.

"That other dude showed up, Broken Skull. All of a sudden, you guys are best buddies. Everything moved so fast. I felt left out … I don't know."

The side of Michael's mouth turned up. "So this isn't about what you did, right? This is about him, now?"

"Michael, I—"

"Shut up. Move on with your story."

"Okay … so, we went in there and held the place up. I looked for Marissa. She was with Markus Doubleday when I found her. I just kind of aired my grievances, I guess. She tried to calm me down."

"He didn't try to stop you?" Michael asked.

Dwight laughed, leaning back and slapping his knee for effect. "Are you kidding me? No. He's soft. S-O-F-T. The softest of the soft. He hightailed it."

Michael wasn't pleased with Dwight's version of the story. He was even less pleased that his little girl conveniently left out the part where Markus left. He thought she was protecting him. Instead, Markus looked like a coward. Michael didn't like cowards.

"Moving on, what got you put in here?" Michael asked.

"The Sound was there. You know, the masked guy?"

"I'm familiar. Go ahead."

"Well, he took out a few of my men. I fought with him, blow for blow. I was getting the upper hand and he grabbed something out of nowhere. Broke my wrist." He showed his wrist to Michael, turning it back and forth. "They had to put some metal in my arm. That ain't no walk in the park."

Michael nodded in agreement with Dwight's words. "I'll bet. Keep going."

"The police showed up. Two minutes, max. All my guys got picked up. I got out of there. I ended up in some alleyway … then, this girl shows up. She's got a mask on too, kinda like The Sound."

"Did you kick her ass and get tripped up later, or what?" Michael asked.

"Depends on how you look at it," Dwight replied.

Michael laughed to himself. He shook his head, annoyed. Shrugging, he said, "How about … the way *you* look at it?"

"I'm in here, ain't I?" Dwight said. There was no other way to explain it, but he didn't want to admit he was stopped and dropped by a girl. He hoped Michael would read between the lines.

Michael leaned forward in his chair and pointed at him. "You know what hurts me? You knew that was my daughter. That's what hurts the most." His voice raised, he said, "It's harder because you're like a son to me. You betrayed my trust, Dwight. That's something earned, and once you get it, it's …"

Michael closed his eyes and slowly shook his head in disgust. When he opened them, his eyes caught Dwight's.

"I'm just very disappointed in you."

Dwight refused to look Michael's way. He wanted to apologize countless times, but understood the finality of his actions. A single tear escaped from each of Dwight's eyes, racing down both his cheeks. The tear on the left finished first, dropping off his jaw and onto his jumpsuit. He heard Michael stand up from his chair.

"Anyway, that's all I need. Thank you for your honesty. Now get up and hug me. We need to move on from this," Michael insisted.

Dwight stood up from the bed. "I meant everything I said. Thank you for coming to see me. Your forgiveness means everything," he said to his mentor.

The two embraced momentarily. Michael placed one of his hands on the back of Dwight's head and pulled him closer. He then laid a kiss on Dwight's forehead and patted the nape of his neck. This time, Dwight couldn't hide his confusion. Michael backed away slowly.

"I would kill for my daughter. Now you know that."

Dwight's face scrunched up with pain. Blood escaped his mouth. He staggered backward. The back of his leg clipped the toilet. He tried to brace himself, collapsing against the wall. Leaning his body against the toilet, his eyes flickered as he panted.

Aside from Dwight's heavy breathing, the prison was still. Michael took a step toward Dwight and pressed his knife against the orange jumpsuit, wiping off both sides until it was clean. He took a step back and stopped. He turned his head slowly toward the Old-Timer.

"Did you see anything?" Michael asked him.

The Old-Timer couldn't take his eyes off Michael, intensely shaking his head no.

"That's what I thought. Look me up when you get out. I might have a job for you."

A stone-faced Michael Buchanan left the cell and walked down the corridor. Putting a gun to his little girl's head was not the smartest – or safest – way to get his attention. Instead of having a conversation about it, Dwight chose to think for himself. As he found out, that wasn't the smartest – or safest – way.

"Quite the surprise," Michael heard behind him.

He turned around. It was Patrick Starks.

"I'll say. Talk about a twist in the end … literally," Emma - Patrick's twin - agreed. They kept their distance behind Michael while they followed him down the corridor.

"I would say he died an honorable death, but the Japanese don't do it like that, I don't think. Something to look up later?"

"Definitely."

Michael stopped in his tracks and turned around. The twins stopped when he did.

"We're done here," Michael said. "Not that I needed you, anyway. I don't know why the Skull sent you."

"Better safe than sorry. It's a good rule of thumb," Emma said, showing Michael her thumb. "And besides … good help is hard to find these days, don't you agree?"

She winked and smiled at him. Michael didn't acknowledge her veiled jab. Instead, he continued his walk down the corridor.

Patrick flicked one of the security doors with his finger, grabbing the attention of an officer just outside it. The three passed through when the officer unlocked the door. Within minutes, they'd left the prison. Right outside the gates, the engine of a black sedan ran. The twins walked toward the car.

"Hey."

The twins stopped, turned, and looked at Michael.

"Next time I get backup … I want the man here, not the help."

Patrick shot Emma a brazen look, one that wondered if Michael Buchanan's words were serious. Emma returned a look to calm him down. Diplomatically, she said, "We'll pass the message on. Hey, do you mind giving us a ride?"

Michael simply shook his head.

The three entered the car. Michael took the passenger's seat. The sedan pulled off into the night. Michael rarely took care of things himself, unless it was a big problem. Dwight Durant was a big problem.

On the other side of town, the Ivory Fox's legs pumped relentlessly. Her feet moved so fast, they skipped on the pavement. Her breaths were shallow and practiced. Her adrenaline rose with every passing step.

"Squirmy … little … chuff!" she muttered under her breath.

Within seconds, she'd gained ground on her target. It wasn't her choice to give him a head start. Luckily for her, he ran down every straightaway he could.

"Stop! Good Lord, will you stop?!"

He refused. He slapped over a garbage can, the contents spilling onto the sidewalk. With less than a second to act, the Fox hurdled it. He turned around twice to look at her. She saw the panic in his eyes and heard it in his breath. He sharply turned a corner and sprinted down another alleyway.

When the Fox turned the corner, her target was farther down the alleyway. Her senses were ablaze, but she continued her chase. Her target was barely a few feet outside the mouth of darkness when, out of nowhere, something crashed in the distance. They both stopped.

Tap … Tap-Tap-Tap-Tap-Tap … Tap-Tap

The Fox threw her hands up and demonstratively shook her head every which way. "Of *course* you'd make a grand entrance." She rolled her eyes, threw her hands on her hips and huffed again. "You just couldn't help yourself, could you?"

The Sound shook his head no.

"Right, then."

Judging by her target's body language, he would not be willfully surrendering. An outbreak of punches and kicks flew the Fox's way. She redirected every attempt with her hands and arms with ease.

Quickly growing bored, the Fox abruptly threw a roundhouse kick that caught her target so fast and hard, it sounded like a hard slap.

Her target stumbled and stopped just short of The Sound, who cocked his fist back. The man's eyes rolled into the back of his head before he dropped to the ground. The two heroes looked down at the Fox's work, then looked up at each other.

"Simple criminals always get the best of me," the Fox confessed.

They heard sirens in the distance, coming fast. The two cocked their heads up when they heard it, then looked at each other again.

"I guess that's our cue, then?" she asked him.

He nodded yes and peeked at his wrist, pushing a couple of buttons. He then waved at the Fox and jumped, his suit was forcefully pulled to the wall, his hands slapping the brick structure. After his feet latched onto the wall, he scaled it with ease, disappearing in seconds.

The Fox's eyes were still following The Sound when she shrugged. "Well ... he's still got it, I suppose." She brought the inside of her wrist to her mouth while she strode out of the alleyway.

"Find me."

She believed she possessed the minimum amount of skills required for her night job. On a good day, she felt on par with The Sound. She knew that deep down, she wasn't. Every day, she felt she learned something new in the classroom and field.

The Fox arrogantly trotted along while she tracked her bike's location. The sirens closing in were a distraction. She felt a time crunch happening, something she was taught to avoid, especially when the police were involved.

Looks like I'm going to have to be artful about this one, she thought.

Vanessa was nearly at the mouth of the alleyway when a police cruiser screeched to a stop. Two more cruisers made three. She sighed and shook her head.

"Freeze! Police!"

Rotating sirens registered in the Fox's eyes. She discreetly looked for a way out. She could risk turning and running, something her partner was proficient in. With her, it never caught on. She raised her hands and stepped forward, careful not to alert the authority.

"Peace first," she murmured. She looked up to the sky. So did they. Grinning, she said, "I hate to do this to the lot of you, because you work *so* hard." The officers drew their guns and approached. She smiled and waved. "Thank you for all you do."

Her bike tightly rounded the corner and screamed down the street. The officers turned, but it was too late. The Fox grabbed the handlebars in stride, feeling the pull and power of the bike when she clamped down.

Her bike accelerated down the street, swiftly approaching top speed. Several gunshots zipped past her. Her best strategy was to guess. The danger scared her until the adrenaline hit. When that happened, being scared became an afterthought.

She hummed a song to stay focused as she made another quick turn, weaving in and out of slower-moving traffic.

Markus won't believe this, she thought.

Back at the scene, the masked man stirred. The kick rocked him, enough that he had to refocus. A pair of boots landed in front of him. When he looked up, he shuddered.

"De La Rosa …"

Dressed in her patented jeans and short leather jacket, De La Rosa peered down at her catch. She squatted down and snatched two fistfuls of his collar, forcing him to his feet. She drove him against the wall, staring at him intensely.

"Scum. You let them get away. That's unfortunate," De La Rosa said. "Because they get to breathe, because they get to be on the street for another night … somebody's gotta pay for this. I'll give you one guess as to who that's going to be."

Daphne looked over at her freshly gathered cohorts, instructing with her eyes. They all nodded and turned their back to her, forming a human wall at the mouth of the alleyway. She turned her attention back to the perpetrator.

Without warning, she threw punch after punch, significant damage done with each blow. He fell back to the concrete and cowered into a ball. Daphne kicked and stomped until she was satisfied. Nostrils flared and breathing heavy, she wiped her mouth with the outside of her hand and started her walk. She took her time down the entire length of the alleyway to adjust her jacket and smooth over her jeans. She strode past the officers.

"Take care of it."

The officers nodded again. She heard their purposeful walk down the alleyway. She promised to clean up the streets. Others were now devoted to her cause. Vigilantes and other scum no longer received a free pass.

Daphne got in her car and pulled away from the hectic scene. She looked in her rear-view mirror. She tucked a few stray strands behind her ear.

"I'm doing the right thing," she whispered to herself.

2

He inspected his bearded face. The patchy areas he struggled to grow in the past were now filled. He stared intensely into the mirror and pointed to his chest.

"Right here. *I* am the one criminals fear at night. *I* can't be stopped. *I* am … without a name."

He crossed his arms across his chest. With gritted teeth, his eyes remained on the mirror as he leaned in.

"Do you have the stones to go out there for the first time tonight? Laugh in the face of danger?"

He blinked. His shoulders slumped.

"Nope. No. Can't do it."

He walked out of the bathroom and plopped on the couch. He'd stopped counting the days he was *this* close to going out and catching bad guys. He wondered how people like The Sound and Ivory Fox built up the courage.

"It's not like I have a whole lot to lose," Jon reasoned. He picked up a couple comic books from his coffee table and carelessly dropped them on the couch. "I have these. Other than that, not much to write home about. Is that my motivation? That I have nothing to lose?"

He flipped the TV on.

"Tomorrow night. That's the night," he promised.

At the Doubleday estate, an unmasked Markus waited in the garage for his partner to arrive. It was nearly 4 a.m., around the time their "shift" ended. Markus was of the opinion that crime actually slept.

3 … 2 … 1 …

He heard the garage door open. The sound of Vanessa's bike speeding down the ramp preceded her arrival. It powered down as she approached. When she hit her parking spot, she parked and swung her leg away from the bike, holding it up while popping out the kickstand. She took off her mask and approached Markus.

"Did that look familiar?" Vanessa grinned.

Markus heaved a sarcastic sigh. "Yes. What you did out there was very impressive. Nice kick."

Vanessa beamed on the inside. She loved to get compliments from Markus, but more so about her field work, as opposed to the work she did at P4P. That was the easy part of her life.

"I didn't even need you!" Vanessa exclaimed. She unzipped her suit. "I mean, I'll always need you, but … you know."

"No, I know."

Even though he'd been a lone wolf during his crime-fighting career, Markus appreciated the company. He always envisioned enlisting future help. As it turned out, he got what he asked for, and more.

He followed her into the bathroom and sat on the counter while she undressed.

"The cops shot at me. *That* was crazy. They had me in a tight situation, but I was able to get out of it, as you see. It seems they've changed their approach, as of late. Have you noticed?"

"I have no doubt they have," Markus replied. "Have they been more aggressive?"

"Quite."

"Do you have concerns?"

Vanessa dramatically blew the air out of her lungs and stared at Markus, fake astonishment slathered all over her face.

"If I did, I wouldn't return after the first time it happened," she said. "I know you're just checking on me, Markus. I just wish you'd get over the fact that you can't get rid of me. It's going to take more to get rid of the Ivory Fox."

She showed him a warm smile.

"What about an army?" he questioned.

She rolled her eyes at him.

He said, "It would definitely take more than that. I'm proud of you, V. You've really picked up all the nuances."

"Oh, don't tell me Markus Doubleday has gone soft," Vanessa cracked. "You've been sentimental with me lately. Is Marissa pregnant, or something?"

With a perturbed look, Markus said, "Absolutely not. I just thought I'd give you some compliments. If you'd like, I could–"

"Oh, no! Please, if you so feel the need to …"

"Just calling it like I see it."

Vanessa tugged at the bottom of her t-shirt and puffed her chest out, then tightened up the string of her pajama pants. She used the reflection of the mirror to look at Markus. "Will that be all, Mr. Doubleday?"

He nodded yes. "That will be all, Ms. Vaughn."

Vanessa slung a small bag over her shoulder and exited the bathroom. Markus followed. They took the familiar ride up to the main level and went their separate ways: Markus, to the kitchen, Vanessa, out the door.

A hurried, cheery voice extended from the kitchen.

"Bye, Vanessa!"

Vanessa softly said, "Good morning and goodbye, Ms. Buchanan."

Marissa's schedule was ironclad: She napped in the early evening to stay up for the six (or so) hours Markus was gone. When he returned, they slept for a few hours before attacking the day together.

She gave him a once-over while her hands ran along the arms of his silk robe. She kissed his cheek.

"I don't know why she's so formal with me," Marissa said. She slid him a bowl of fruit salad.

"Maybe just being respectful?" Markus guessed, digging into his food.

"I don't know … probably," Marissa said. "Any boo-boos?"

With a full mouth, he said, "No boo-boos."

"Good to hear. As much as the streets don't want to deal with The Sound, I'm sure they don't want to deal with … Mare Bear."

Markus stopped chewing. He raised an eyebrow. "Mare Bear?"

Marissa smirked. "Just something I came up with. That'd be my name, should I decide to dedicate my whole life to righting wrongs. The 'Bear' part just means I'm fierce, hungry, and I sleep a lot. Now that I think of it, I don't know if that's a good idea for a name."

"It's not a good idea," Markus assured, finishing up his fruit salad. "We'll find a name for you eventually. You do too much in the world not to have one."

Marissa held her hands on her heart. "I won't argue. When you're right, you're right," she said. "Your compliments are rolling off the tongue. Do you think I'm pregnant or something?"

"Vanessa asked me the same thing. Great minds, I guess," Markus said dryly. He washed his bowl out and placed it in the dishwasher, heading to the stairs. Marissa walked beside him.

"Well, you reward good work, it's just … lately, you've been very compliment-y."

"Maybe I'm softening, in my old age."

Markus pushed the master bedroom door open, wiggling free of his robe soon after. When they both crawled into bed, he turned his back to her. Marissa intertwined her fingers and rested them right below her chest. She found herself staring at the ceiling.

"Goodnight, Mare," Markus said.

"Goodnight."

"I love you."

"I love you, too."

When night turned to morning, another familiar face rose.

Slowly pushing off his blankets, Jasper Kane lazily sat up. The knots on his back were concrete evidence of the couch being nothing but a nuisance. When Jasper's bare feet hit the carpeted floor, his hands took turns rubbing the opposite arm; the goosebumps went away with his warm touch. He grabbed his t-shirt and slid it on, then knocked on the nearby door and opened it.

"Good morning."

The comforter rustled and she slowly stirred, emerging out of the pleasant confines.

"And good morning to you," Vanessa replied. "Apologies for the sleeping arrangements."

"When are you going to stop apologizing?" Jasper questioned. "I know the setup when I come over. It's the same when you sleep at my place. It's no big deal, I just want to make sure you're comfortable with the arrangements."

Vanessa shrugged and said, "Well, thank you for understanding."

Dressed in tights and a t-shirt, she slid out of bed and headed to the bathroom. Jasper averted his eyes. She didn't stress about whether Jasper was looking or not. He thought she was beautiful, one of the rare ones able to wake up in the morning and go. No makeup or maintenance needed.

"Are we still on for dinner?" Jasper asked, his voice popping through the door.

"Unless something comes up, I would assume so," she responded, wiggling in and out of clothes.

"Let me ask you something: Do you actually believe in that whole, 'Success before Rest' thing your boss pushes?"

Vanessa opened the bathroom door. "I believe it with my whole heart."

She walked to the kitchen and rummaged through her near-bare pantry. "There are some that rest before achieving success, and God help them. As far as the tagline goes, Mr. Doubleday is the example." She tossed a couple breakfast bars to Jasper and grabbed a couple for herself.

"So we've been dating a few months now," Jasper said. He took a bite of his breakfast bar. "Even though we're still feeling each other out, I'm comfortable with you. I don't want to show my cards too early, but … I really like you, Vanessa."

Jasper's hesitant words drew a smile from Vanessa. "Oh, I easily feel the same way, Mr. Kane. You've intrigued me since the day we met at that bar. I'd say you won me over." She finished one of her breakfast bars and opened the other.

Vanessa's words were music to Jasper's ears. Even with all the chaos he caused as the Broken Skull, he justified it by constantly reminding himself of all the "normal" things he did: He helped people, he was charitable, and he was involved in a steady relationship.

She makes me want to be a better person. I feel warm inside when she smiles. With all the positive things she brings to the table, why do I still do what I do?

"I won you over? Glad to hear it," Jasper said. "I was starting to wonder."

She playfully narrowed her eyes at him.

"Don't look at me like that," Jasper said. "You know how I feel about you doing that."

Vanessa laughed at him. "It's because you think I'm sexy, right?" she asked. "It's got to be the accent, I'm sure of it."

"Yes." He took a bite of his breakfast bar. "To your accent, could not be more untrue."

"Is it because you get to sleep on a couch in your jeans when you're around me?"

"I don't have to, I *get* to," he corrected. He leaned in and kissed her on the cheek. She craned her neck in a way to expose her cheek more. He kissed her again.

"What's going on at the old loony bin?" Vanessa asked.

"Oh, you know … loony things," Jasper responded. "Speaking of, I'm going to be doing some radio work later. Just spreading the message that what people think is best isn't always best, and so on and so forth. It's a never-ending process, right? Getting this world right?"

Jasper's words struck a chord with Vanessa. She'd been working to get the world right, one night at a time. It was good that someone understood what the world needed. She didn't know if she would ever know Jasper well enough to tell him she was the Ivory Fox, but she could definitely see it trending that way, especially since Markus told Marissa.

Wait, but Markus has known Marissa for a very long while. Do I have to wait 20-whatever years? Is it a feeling I get? Will I know when it's the right time? I'm over-thinking this, I think.

All she said was, "I suppose."

"Do you really have to suppose?" Jasper said.

"I suppose n– …" she laughed when she caught herself. "No."

"You have the potential for more great things," Jasper said. "You're currently assisting a man who impacts the world like few before him. Who knows where you'll be in a year? Two years? Five years? You could end up with more influence than he."

If you only knew.

3

"No mas!"

After a night of ridding the streets of criminal activity, the alarm clock's blare signaled the end of De La Rosa's sleep. She turned off her annoying alarm, opened up her phone and started playing a podcast she wanted to finish.

"So, Jasper … what do you think of all this hoopla surrounding The Sound and … is it … Ivory Fox?"

"Correct," Jasper said. "Regarding the hoopla – as you put it – it's good for a story. The media needs something all the time now, it seems. What better story than this?"

"Right. I mean, it's gotta look bad for the cops, right?"

"I believe so. It makes them appear incompetent, which couldn't be further from the truth. I'm a huge advocate for the police. Since their quest is to bring The Sound and Ivory Fox to justice, I will advocate for that. For purely selfish purposes, I want to personally analyze those two, see what makes them tick."

"That's what the world needs, powerful advocates. You have any opinions about the Broken Skull?" the caller asked.

"What *about* the Broken Skull?"

"You wanna talk about a terrorist … he hijacked a signal and actually got T.V. time!" the host responded, sounding appalled.

"People talk about The Sound and Ivory Fox being a menace to society. Wouldn't the Broken Skull be more of one?"

"Absolutely agree," Jasper said. "Tell me how this works: The heroes are helping the cops, who hate them. The heroes are trying to bring down the Broken Skull, a menace that's been wreaking havoc on this city for too long. The cops hate him, too. The Broken Skull wants to bring down everyone, from the looks of it."

Laughing, the host said, "The craziest triangle I ever heard of."

"It's definitely not normal," Jasper admitted. "People will win or lose in situations like this … it's just a matter of how much."

"Changing gears, we're going to t–"

Daphne changed the channel to a "Today's Hits" station. She didn't want to get too riled up before work. She bobbed her head along with the tunes while readying herself for the day. She felt compelled to look in the mirror. For the first time in a long time, she felt she could look at her reflection and respect what she saw.

After she got herself out the house and to the precinct, Daphne walked through the doors.

"Cap wants to see you," one of the detectives said.

She nodded sarcastically when she passed. "Of course he does."

She knocked when she arrived at the door. No answer. She turned the knob and pushed the door open, looking around office. "He's not even in here," she muttered.

She settled in one of the seats across from the Captain's empty chair. She tapped on the arms of her chair, staring blankly at the leather in front of her.

In less than a minute, the office door swung open. Daphne turned her head. It was Captain Grove. She stood up.

"Captain."

"Lieutenant."

Her neck cocked back. She tucked her chin and raised her eyebrows. "Lieutenant?"

"You interested?" Grove asked.

Nodding her head up and down, she said, "Yes. I'm sorry, I just … wasn't expecting a promotion when I walked in today."

Captain Grove said, "Daphne, you've been impressive lately. Your dedication deserves a reward."

"Okay, well thank you, sir."

"I also know what you've been doing in the streets."

Daphne's heart rate raised.

How much does he know? How much is he actually okay with? Is he promoting me to keep me behind a desk and off the streets?

Instead of overthinking, she pursed her lips and said, "What do you mean?"

"Ramping up your efforts to stop the vigilante problem we have," Grove said. "I've noticed. This Sound and Fox thing is a little of an obsession for you, I think."

Self-consciousness dripped into Daphne's veins. She avoided eye contact with him for a few moments. When she collected her thoughts, she looked his way.

"Can I just be honest with you?" Daphne asked Grove. She didn't wait for his answer. "I want to put a stop to it. We should take back the streets. I'm tired of this city wondering who's really in charge. When we're done, I don't want to leave any question."

Groves grabbed his chin, his hand covering most of his mouth. "What exactly are you saying?" he asked.

"I want D.O.A. rules," Daphne said. "I want to take them all out, one way or another. If we bring them in alive? Good. If we bring them back in a body bag … whatever. Circumstances happen."

His hand still covering his mouth, Captain Grove blinked a few times and raised his eyebrows. "You're serious about this."

"Dead," she said.

"You have my authorization," Captain Grove said, "but I don't want to hear about it. Just so we're clear, if you get caught by any of the higher-ups, I'll deny this meeting ever happened. You'll burn with your beliefs. You better be *damn* sure you know what you're getting yourself into."

Daphne nodded her head with conviction. "Yes sir, I do. Thank you so much for this opportunity. I won't let you down."

"Just take care of it," he said dismissively.

At Coleman's – the place Markus ordered food from frequently – Jasper and Vanessa had just accepted their respective dinners. Because of the amount of times she'd eaten there, it was an easy go-to for Vanessa. Jasper didn't mind much when it came to food, so the choice was simple. Jasper held up his glass.

"To … getting what we want out of this life."

"Agree," Vanessa said. "I'm sorry I have nothing extravagant in this glass," she said, lightly clanging her glass against his. "The last thing I need is to feel tipsy."

"I'll drink a glass. I'll say we split it," Jasper said nonchalantly. Vanessa smiled and kept her lips on her glass, sipping slowly. She peered at Jasper over her glass. His eyes were already on her.

He didn't know how much longer he could hide his secret from her. It was a constant battle, made worse by their time spent together. One day, he feared a moment of vulnerability might cost him everything.

"I'm going against my better judgment by discussing this, but there are some crazy people out there in this world," Jasper said. "The things I hear in my office would make me fall out of my chair, if I wasn't ready. Then again, spending a night like this with you makes all the crazy worth it."

Jasper's words made Vanessa's cheeks warm. With her fork, she stabbed into her food and took a bite, chewing several times before swallowing. When she was done, she cleared her throat. The rosy-colored cheeks had disappeared.

"There isn't as much excitement over at P4P as there is in your office, but the little time I get to have a rest with you … it's pretty fantastic. Forgive me for changing the subject, but how'd the radio thing go?"

He cocked his head and blinked simultaneously. "Oh, speaking of crazy … on that podcast I recorded, we talked about all the vigilantism going on around the city, specifically, the Broken Skull. I'm sorry, I just think he's a nut job. My professional opinion? There's no helping him."

"Indeed," Vanessa said. She pointed to her temple and said, "Something about that man's real screwy up here."

Jasper rubbed his chin. He hadn't touched his food since they delivered it. Vanessa was used to it: Anytime they engaged in good conversation, he dropped everything and focused on her words. He bothered with very little else.

"Besides the obvious, why do you think he's so … screwy, as you put it?" Jasper asked.

"Oh, I don't know, Jasper. I'm just chatting you up," Vanessa said. "Anyone who gets on TV and talks about taking a whole city down, especially since I have the sneaking suspicion that he didn't pay for that TV time, it's just screwy … as I put it."

They both shared a chuckle. He was sure her sarcasm was a social cue.

"The whole lot of this just seems so absurd to me," Vanessa said. "I think the idea of people dressing up in abnormal clothing, doing abnormal things … I bet you'd love for *those* people to walk into your office," she chuckled again. "They're all going to be brought down, I think. It's really just a matter of when."

"You think so?"

"I do."

"Agreed."

The two dug into their food, trading glances along the way. Vanessa was almost done. She was more equipped to eat and carry on a conversation. She was also of the opinion that she needed to keep her identity under wraps. The last thing she wanted was for Jasper to think she was crazy, or for anything to happen to him because of her. He surely wouldn't understand her cause, would he?

On the other side of town, hard, rapid knocks on his apartment door brought Jonathan Deadmarsh out of his slumber. He held his chest. His heart rate felt like a million beats a minute. He stretched his fingers out and rested them on his chest.

"Oh God. I almost died, I'm sure." He exhaled and looked at the door. "God." He stood up and ambled over, checking the peephole.

It was De La Rosa. Her brow was furrowed. In the past, she would knock a couple rounds. If he didn't answer, she would leave. This time, she took a step back and stood in the hallway, breathing heavily. She looked frustrated, to him. He held his breath and stood still.

"I heard you walk to the door, Deadmarsh. Open up," she demanded. Her voice sounded close to the door.

Jon remained still.

"I'm going to shoot your doorknob if you don't open the door," Daphne threatened.

A few seconds later, he cracked the door open, just enough to show his head. "To be clear, I only opened the door because I want my deposit back when I move."

Daphne looked him up and down. "You been working out?"

With a distant look in his eye, he said, "A little."

She looked him up and down again. "Well, you look good."

"Thank you." The smallest smile escaped his features.

"Can I come in, or do you have company, or something? Looks like you're trying to hide something." A nervous laugh mingled with her words. Jon's smile faded. He stood up taller.

"What do you need, Detective."

Daphne's smile skittered away. He called her Detective, making the conversation formal. She didn't want formal.

"I'm actually a Lieutenant now," she said. "I just want to talk to my friend ... or at least, someone I think of as a friend."

"Lieutenant? Wow. Okay, well ... what do you want to talk about?"

Daphne slid her hands in her pockets and looked away for a moment. When her eyes returned, she said, "I just had a lot of time to think, and ... can I come in for five minutes? It's weird talking to you in the hallway."

Jon stared through Daphne when he said, "I don't know."

"Five minutes," Daphne begged. "I'll leave in five minutes."

"Five minutes," Jon asserted.

He opened the door. When she came in, she stood in his living room and took in its familiarity: The look and the smell brought an unexplained comfort, a feeling she couldn't get anywhere else.

"Not much has changed," she commented.

"It hasn't been that long," he shot back. "So, is this murder by small-talk, or …"

Daphne hid her disdain for Jon's current approach. Her anger would blow the conversation to smithereens. Her tone was flat when she said, "I just want to know what you've been up to nowadays. Anything new? New job?"

"I don't know yet," Jon said. "Maybe I'll become a teacher or something. Luckily, I can sit on the huge pile of money I saved from being a detective. Since I had no friends and never went out, there were lots of opportunities to save."

Daphne ignored his comment, looking around the apartment. Everything had a place, a far cry from months ago, when she last visited. "This is probably the cleanest I've ever seen your apartment, Jon. Jesus."

Jon looked around the apartment alongside her. "If you had as much time as I had, your house would be immaculate, too. I mean, yours is clean, but not 'unemployed' clean."

Daphne pressed her lips together and tried not to smile. It didn't work. "I miss you," she slipped. She closed her eyes and looked away, shaking her head once to the left and right.

Jon's sole focus was on Daphne's words. His response was swift. "Daphne … don't. Just don't."

She looked at him. "I can't help it. I 've been here a few hundred times since we fell out. I tried to let it go, but … I guess I just don't want to fight my feelings anymore. Listen: I thought about it, and I'm willing to look past your beliefs about all the things happening on the street."

Jon outwardly showed his dismay.

"You're willing to look past the fact that we're not on the same side on a – let's face it – pretty big topic? That's like trying to be in a relationship, despite having extremely opposite religious and political beliefs."

"So it's clear we're not going to be in a relationship. I get that," she said. "But I like talking to you, and I don't want to lose you completely. I don't have a lot of people I'm close with."

Jon stopped to think for a moment, gathered his words and said, "Okay, so wc can talk, but that one topic is not up for discussion. We can't agree on that, and never will. I think friends is okay."

"Yeah, that works," Daphne said. "Oh yeah, one more thing before we close the book on that subject: Captain Grove's talking about taking back the streets. More 'By Any Means Necessary' than 'Serve and Protect.'"

Jon's ears perked up. He looked at Daphne. The worry on her face rendered his tough-talk useless. "Daph, I'm not with the

Force anymore," he reminded her. "I mean, thanks for thinking about me, but … what does any of this have to do with me?"

"I'm telling you because …" she paused, gathered her thoughts and continued. "Because I know you're rooting for the Sound guy and his buddy."

Jon was confused. "You came to tell me this – I'm just guessing here – because you think I can warn them, somehow?"

Daphne shrugged and exhaled. "God, Jon, I don't know. I feel like if anyone would know where they'd pop up, it'd be you. You know this stuff like the back of your hand. You're a smart guy. I bet you could guess their next move without trying."

Jon ran his fingers through his tangled hair, his fingers fighting through all the knots. "So, Grove said he wants to take the streets back?"

"Yes," Daphne said. "He even talked about killing them." Her last few words were no higher than a whisper. Her gaze found her knees. She rubbed her hands on her jeans to get rid of the perspiration.

He couldn't hide his feelings about Daphne's revelation. He never thought Grove would resort to that desperate way of thinking. How could someone carelessly throw someone else's life away like that? Then, it hit him.

"What side do *you* fall on?"

Daphne looked up, finding Jon's eyes. "I think you know the answer to that."

Jon raised his eyebrows slightly. "Even after you hear that lunacy, you're like, 'Yeah, that makes sense' when you know it doesn't?"

"It's the right thing to do," she said. "They don't know any better. It's up to us to restore order and keep the peace."

"Are you listening to yourself right now?!" Jon asked. "You're not talking about arresting people; you're talking about *killing* people, Daphne. You're talking about killing people you *know* are trying to make a difference. They're risking their lives to help, as it is. They don't need another enemy."

They'd reached a stalemate, the story of their former partnership. Before Daphne got too emotional – there was something she didn't like about how Jon made her feel – she stood up from the couch and strode toward the door.

"What if I was out there?" he blurted out.

Daphne stopped. Jon swallowed hard. She turned around.

"*Were* you out there?" she asked in a threatening tone, narrowing her eyes and slowly closing the door back. He felt the small hairs on the back of his neck stand up.

"I've considered it," Jon said. "And you never answered my question."

"I'm only going to tell you this once, Deadmarsh," she said. "If I see you out there trying to be a hero, like all those other idiots, or helping them in any way …" she pointed out the window behind him for effect.

"I won't hesitate to take you down."

Her spine-tingling words seeped in as she slammed Jon's apartment door. He waited a half-minute before forcing himself up from the couch to lock the door. He grabbed his phone and thumb-punched the screen rapidly, tossing his phone on the couch when he finished.

Deep down, Jon wished he could pull some decency out of her. Instead, she only got madder at his words.

4

"We can spar, right?"

"We can, but only for about 5, 10 minutes. We have work this morning."

"Oh, don't remind me of such things, Markus. You can really damper a girl's day quite quickly."

"It's my job to damper your day. Maybe I should stop being The Sound. Maybe I should call myself the Wet Blanket."

While she laughed, Vanessa said, "Good show." She then took her mask off and tossed it to the ground. "Shall we?"

Markus tossed his mask. With Vanessa's next breath, she threw a stiff jab at Markus. He dodged.

"Whoa!" he said, cracking a smile.

She returned his sentiment, starting to circle. "I told you I'm ready!" she said, weaving head movement with shoulder fakes. "I'm feeling very frisky. In fact, so frisky that I'm going to hit you tonight."

"Oh, tonight's the night? What's so special about tonight?" Markus asked, also circling.

"What's special? Didn't you hear me, dear Markus? Tonight will mark the first time in the history of our sparring that I hit you!"

Before Markus could come back with clever words, Vanessa unleashed a head kick. He blocked it clean and threw a punch. She grabbed his wrist and flipped him. He landed on his feet, grabbed her wrist and flipped her. She landed clean and threw a hard roundhouse kick, just like the one in the alley. He ducked and pushed her in the back. She stumbled, but quickly caught her footing. She turned and faced him. His grin was ear-to-ear.

She shook her head in disbelief. He'd gotten the best of her numerous times in the past. He also knew how much that smile got under her skin.

"Good warm-up," Vanessa said. "Here we go."

She attempted to head butt him and missed. Her rage rose as she threw a back elbow, followed by another roundhouse. She came up short. She sprung on her hands and mule kicked him. He caught her legs and ran forward. She kicked free and spun around, facing him.

She blew air out of her lungs and stood up. "God, you have to be such a Jessie."

"Did you just call me a girl?" Markus asked.

"You've been brushing up on your slang?"

"I read, here and there."

"I bet if the tables were turned, I could say all the cool things."

"Consider the tables turned."

He rushed her. Three consecutive kicks came her way: One low, one middle and one high. She blocked all three. She threw a punch to create space between them. The two were in the middle of catching their breath when she let a smirk escape. He smirked back.

He charged her, tackled her to the ground, and mounted her. Her legs split open and wrapped around his torso. He threw two punches at her face. She dodged them. He threw another. She grabbed his wrist and sprung her hips up, locking her legs around his head. She arched her back to increase pressure.

The initial squeeze caught him by surprise. With his free hand, he grabbed her head and pulled up on it, ripping his arm free. He took a couple steps back.

Her breath laboring, she slowly stood up. Her hands on her hips, she asked, "Does that count? I felt panic."

"No, it doesn't," Markus said.

"Oh, keep it!" Vanessa cried, legitimately upset at the ruling. "I may not have hit you in the technical sense, but I *did* get the best of you, for an itty-bitty second. You have to admit that!" she added, pinching her forefinger and thumb together. "Just a little."

Markus remained proud.

"From a technical standpoint, you didn't hit me," he told her. She nodded her head in agreement. "You weren't successful with any of your strikes."

"But?"

He sighed. "But … you *did* get the best of me, for an itty-bitty moment," he confessed, mocking Vanessa's mannerisms.

"See? I knew you weren't some insufferable, sexist bum!" Vanessa celebrated. She lunged and tightly embraced him.

Insufferable, sexist bum? People think of me that way?

Arms still around his neck, Vanessa pulled back from the hug. Silence fell between them as they looked at each other. The attraction between them was difficult to understand, difficult to explain. They were both in relationships, yet they found it hard to co-exist in close proximity.

A cleared throat was a welcome distraction.

"Am I interrupting something?" Marissa asked, innocence in her tone.

"No. Nothing big," Markus said. He raised his shoulders, an effort to remind Vanessa that her arms were still draped around him. She quickly pulled her arms off his neck and placed them tight by her side.

"He may not want to admit it, but I just had him in quite the compromising position," she cheerily said to Marissa. She pointed at him and said, "Don't let him tell you different!"

Marissa looked at Markus. Markus looked at Vanessa.

"I don't own a knife, but I know what I'd cut this tension with," Vanessa said. "Excuse me."

Vanessa walked to the changing bathroom and shut the door.

"Are you ready to go upstairs?" Marissa asked.

"Sure, let's go. Vanessa will be fine down here," he answered.

They both boarded the platform and headed up to the main level without saying a word to each other. Markus shed every bit of Sound-related clothing and substituted it for a pair of silk pajamas.

The prior scene certainly left a bad taste in Marissa's mouth. She didn't want to overreact, but she was curious. The worst thing – to her – was to let it fester and get worse.

When their bedroom door shut, Markus pulled the comforter up and slid in, stretching the comforter up to his neck, his back to Marissa.

"No shower?" Marissa questioned.

"I'm tired. I'll take one when I wake up," Markus responded.

"So, Vanessa says she got the best of you."

"She did."

"Care to explain? I kind of feel like, in the dark."

Markus shifted over and faced an undressing Marissa. "We were sparring. We have this running bet that she can't hit me."

"So, what's with the compromising position, then?"

"She tried to choke me."

"Oh … good for her, right?"

"Yeah. She would've gotten anyone else."

"Like, choked them?"

"Yes, Mare." Markus said.

Knowing him, Marissa smelled his forceful and agitated tone coming a mile away. Annoyed, she said, "Can you tell me what's bothering you, or is this something I should leave alone?"

Markus rolled to his back and looked at the ceiling. Marissa slid in bed beside him.

"She's better than me," Markus acknowledged. "She's like I was, when I started. Just … fire. She's so aggressive, so thorough.

She takes so many notes. She's going to be better than I ever was. We have the same common bond - with our parents' murder - but she's better."

He sighed.

"I should be happier. I'm her teacher. I should be celebrating how good she's gotten. Instead, I'm complaining about it. I don't know if I've gotten complacent. I just wish I knew."

"As much as I'd like to stay up and be mad with you about your embarrassment of riches, I think I'm going to turn in," Marissa told Markus. She smiled and nuzzled next to him, getting comfortable on his arm. He sighed again.

"I'm not going to be able to sleep if you keep doing that," she half-joked. "Get some sleep. You'll have a clearer mind in the morning."

Was Markus losing his edge? Was Marissa jealous about Markus and Vanessa's dynamic? As they were finding out, there were more things to think about than their relationship. The one constant was what The Sound brought to both their lives.

That could also be perceived as the root of the problem.

In his office the next morning, Markus sifted through digital paperwork, rapidly moving the bits of information to their respective places with his hands. There was a knock at the door.

"Come in, Vanessa."

He briefly studied her and went back to his work. She moved to shut the door.

"Please keep the door open."

Vanessa raised her eyebrows, then lifelessly shrugged. He never asked her to do that before. This was new. "Of course I can, absolutely."

It still mesmerized her how quickly Markus read and discarded information. It surprised her that he was able to retain all that information while never mismanaging a file. He was definitely a special talent, to her.

"Sir, if it's none of my business, then say so, but ... is everything right with you?"

"Yes, everything's fine."

"Sir, if I'm not being too pushy, can you stop for a moment?"

"I haven't stopped in years. Computer, save my progress and sleep."

All the holograms disappeared. He looked at her, rubbing his hands to keep busy. "What can I do for you, Ms. Vaughn?"

"I noticed you didn't hug me back when I hugged you last night. Is it because Ms. Buchanan was there?"

"I don't really know, Ms. Vaughn," Markus answered.

He knew. He was competitive. She got the best of him, even if it was for a split-second. If someone out in the field got the best of him, it could cost him his life. He was thankful it was only Vanessa.

"But I will say, you've gotten so much better. It's night and day, from a few months ago," Markus told her.

Vanessa fought the urge to smile. Instead, she dipped her head and hid the excitement.

"With all due respect, I have a lot more to learn," Vanessa said, downplaying Markus's words. "I want to be as good as you. That'll take heaps of experience. Maybe one day, I can train someone, like you trained me. Maybe you won't have to do this forever."

"Is there a forever for you?" Vanessa asked.

I need to be okay with saying this.

"Well…" Markus searched for the right words to say. Nodding, he said, "No, this won't last forever."

He imagined the discomfort of an athlete talking about having to retire in their prime.

"There are all kinds of reasons, I think. You can get too old for it, you can have a traumatic experience that pushes you out, or you can get killed doing it … and another: You can retire early, of sound body and mind."

Vanessa thought about Markus's words. The way he was so calm, The Sound fit perfectly. She wondered if he was too calm.

"What would you like to see happen? You don't seem convinced," Markus said.

Vanessa rested her index finger on her chin, deep in thought. She raised an eyebrow and shrugged again.

"Down the road, having a family sounds really nice," Vanessa said. "I want to see an end to crime and violence, but I fear that's wishful thinking."

She pondered.

"I don't want to die doing this, but I full-well know the risks. I'm going to keep doing it, but I want to come out happy with the legacy we're building … or have built, in your case. Plus, I've started a new relationship. I'd like to see where it goes, before it's all said and done."

Markus furrowed his brow. He felt jealousy creep in. "Who's the lucky guy?"

"Jasper Kane."

"Oh. I know of him more than I actually know him," Markus said. "He's the, um … therapist, right?"

"He is," Vanessa answered. She didn't know why she felt so nervous telling Markus that. True to form, she didn't see a reaction from Markus.

"Sounds great. It looks like he hasn't interfered with your nightly work."

"Oh, no. He's been unknowingly cooperative."

Markus nodded. "And a gentleman?"

"Like you wouldn't believe," she smiled.

Her thoughts warmed her up. It also warmed her to know that Markus looked out for her personally and professionally.

"That's what I like to hear," Markus said. "If you encounter a time where you feel uncomfortable, let me know. I have a friend."

"If I ever feel uncomfortable, you might not get there quick enough," Vanessa smirked. "He's really no trouble, indubitably a sweetheart."
"Sounds good," Markus said. "Do you need anything else?"

"I don't think I require anything else," Vanessa replied. "Cheers."

Markus returned to his work. Vanessa left. Another arrived.

"Hey."

Markus let out a brief sigh. Being stopped in the middle of work for the second time in a matter of minutes left him frustrated. He tried not to show it, but slipped. Markus bunched the holograms up and made them disappear by clasping his hands.

"Hey Mare."

"Hey, I was just … can I close this door?"

"Yes, of course."

Marissa walked over to Markus and pecked him lightly on the lips. He didn't peck her back with as much energy. It was then that she decided it would be a short stay.

"I know you wouldn't cheat on me, it's just … things are weird right now," Marissa stated. "I saw Vanessa hugging you, and I freaked. I don't know what came over me. I know I shouldn't be acting like this, I just thought this whole 'night job' would be a lot lighter."

"So what's your play, then? Are you saying you don't want to do this? I'm confused," Markus said.

"Are *you* trying to say that?" Marissa snapped.

"Let me be clear, Mare: I'm in love with you. I also understand why it would be so complicated for you."

"Do you *really* understand? Honey, I don't think you do. And frankly, I'm a little insulted that you're downplaying my feelings."

"Okay. Why don't we just take some time to figure out what we're trying to say?" Markus suggested. "We don't have to talk about this right now. Tensions are high, and I don't want to fight."

Marissa knew Markus wasn't feeding her a line to shut her up. She knew he was about efficiency; he wouldn't lose his composure when it came to affairs of the heart. Sometimes, he came off as robotic to her. She'd take that over a meltdown.

"Markus, I know you're going to be busy at night, like every night. Please just promise me we'll talk before you go out tonight."

"Mare, I promise we'll talk tonight. I'm always busy, but I've always made time for you."

"I know, it's just … it can wait. It can definitely wait. I'll see you when you get home."

They both pecked each other on the lips before she walked out the door. Markus found himself alone again. He knew he was capable of juggling his life, he just had to manage his time better.

Resolutions were on the horizon: A smoother relationship with Marissa, a better relationship with Vanessa, and the beginning of a relationship with the Broken Skull. He opened his holograms and resumed work.

"What am I looking at?"

"What am I looking at?" Emma repeated to Patrick. "All kinds of things. Surfing the internet … you know, the thing you do when you're bored?"

"Oh, Emma … so abrasive," Patrick said, nodding. "There's really no need for that, you know. You've really been into your phone lately. Care to share?"

In a light tone, she said, "No, I don't."

Patrick shrugged. "Okay, but you're forcing me to use my Twin Powers on you. I'll just read your mind."

Patrick narrowed his eyes and pressed his index and middle fingers to his temples, staring intently at Emma. Instead of looking away, she stared right back at Patrick, both of them failing to blink. Within seconds, his mouth formed an o-shape.

"What?" Emma asked.

"You like a boy!" Patrick exclaimed.

"You couldn't be more wrong, sweet Patty-Cake."

"I don't think I am, but if you say so."

"Well, I say so. Where would I find the time for that? Plus, must I remind of you of the things we do? I'm afraid I couldn't afford to have someone knowing the real me."

"Well, you *do* have a point," Patrick stated. "Have you heard from the Broken Skull?"

"Not in days," Emma answered, playing with a few strands of her hair.

Patrick raised his eyebrows, shook his head no, and blinked hard before opening his eyes again.

"I'm not into standing pat. Maybe we should seek him out?" he wondered. "I've already made up my mind, I just want to hear your take."

"I'm sure we'll run into him. It doesn't take much. Just go where the chaos is, right?" Emma smiled. Patrick matched her smile, patted her leg and left her bedroom.

Again, Emma got lost in her thoughts.

That Deadmarsh boy was as close to a regular boy as I've been around in a long, long time. Maybe he's the most accessible, is why I'm obsessing? I wonder what it would be like to have normalcy. It doesn't hurt that he's cute.

It does hurt that my brother punched him out, however.

5

Night fell.

Marissa pulled into the driveway of the home she shared with Markus. She rested her head on her seat's leather headrest and closed her eyes.

Am I capable of sitting back and letting things happen to me, especially when they directly affect me? I need to tell him how I feel, and he needs to do the same. He's not leaving this house until we hash it out. I don't care how long Vanessa has to wait.

Marissa stepped out of the car and into the house. Her eyes landed on Markus, who was sitting on the couch. To her, it looked like he was waiting.

"Hey," she said sheepishly.

Markus patted the couch cushion next to him. "Hey. Come sit. Get comfortable."

She sat, crossing her legs toward him. She rested the side of her head and shoulder on the back cushion.

"So, are–"

"Yes, Markus. We have to talk about this."

"I was afraid of that," he said. He cocked his head to the side. "What's *really* on your mind, Marissa?"

Marissa found it hard to hide her displeasure. He usually called her Mare. Was he frustrated? She tried not to concern herself with it. She had to get her feelings out, or it could get worse.

Her voice was barely above a whisper when she said, "I don't know if we moved too fast, or …"

Markus's ears perked up. He didn't expect those words. He pushed up from the couch and sat up straight, keeping his hands firmly planted. "Well, what makes you think that?" was all he could muster.

"I think I tried to blame Vanessa in the beginning. The truth is, maybe I should've thought more in-depth," Marissa said. "I was in such a rush to get back home and be with you. I didn't weigh the pros and cons of being with you *and* The Sound. I mean, that's what it is, right? If I want to be with you, I have to be with The Sound?"

Markus remained tight-lipped while he dissected her thoughts and formulated his own. Finally, he came up with something that made sense to him.

He sighed and said, "I can't make you stay. I'd like it if you did, but I can't hold you hostage. You're definitely appreciated, loved immensely … but you knew this was a package deal. You knew what you were getting into as soon as I told you about it. The speed we went is irrelevant."

"Yeah, I-I know … I'm just saying, though: It's harder than I convinced myself it was. You're so busy fighting other people's battles, I think it's clouded your perception of the one right here."

"That's a great point," Markus countered, "but I can't stop."

"Well, I don't mean to go all, 'I'm a five-year old,' but why?" Marissa cried. "Why can't you just cut it off? Because of you, crime in this city is low. Look, I understand that it fills a void in your life. I know I can't be everything for you, but … I thought I helped with that, you know?"

He put his hand on her knee. "It does. Don't get me wrong. Your presence renews me, like I can impact the world even more than I already do."

She rested her hand on top of his. "So, what you're saying is, it's not enough, right? Isn't that what you're saying?"

Markus paused. Marissa's moment of clarity scared him. He wondered if he needed people, in the traditional sense. He wondered if his concept of normal was skewed. Instead of sitting inside his own head, Markus spoke.

"I think that's what I'm saying. I'm sorry. I haven't done enough. I don't know when enough will be, but I'm certain I'll know when the time comes. It's not that I've changed the way I feel about you, so–"

"So maybe I should just move out and give you the space you need?" Marissa interrupted. Exasperated, she said, "This is obviously important to you, at least, more important than what we have going on."

"Wait a minute," Markus abruptly warned. "I wouldn't say that The Sound is *so* much more important than what we have going on, it's j–"

"It's just … what it is, Markus. Let it go. I'm not super mad, or anything. You probably just need time. I'm sure Vanessa's waiting for you downstairs," she said quickly, changing the subject. The more they talked about it, the more her emotions showed.

"Okay, well …" Markus was at a loss for words. He pushed up from the couch. "Are we just friends now, or am I reading this situation wrong? I don't really know what we're doing, here."

Marissa stood up, as well. "Let's just work on it," she suggested. "That's all I got right now. If you want to work on it, let's work on it. We can still do business together, I'm assuming. That's still important to you, right? Money?"

Her words stung. He scrunched up his face and grimaced.

"This is exactly what I wanted to avoid," he said. They barely brushed each other's shoulders as he passed. She turned around and watched him walk toward the basement. He placed his hand on the sensor.

"It may not be today, but one day, we'll have our Happily Ever After," Marissa said confidently. "But you have to meet me halfway. Oh! And before you leave, I forgot to tell you: We're having a party soon."

Markus's eyebrows sloped. "How soon are we talking?"

Marissa shrugged awkwardly and smiled, her hands up and out. "Tomorrow night?"

Markus dramatically blew all the air out of his system. "Okay. Short notice, but doable. Just let me know what you need."

When he shut the basement door, Marissa plunked down on the couch, closed her eyes and rubbed her temples.

I just want a normal life. Is that too much to ask? I don't want to sleep every night by myself, just because my boyfriend needs his adrenaline fix, or whatever's going on in that pretty little head of his.

"Ugh … stupid love," she said out loud.

Downstairs, Markus had three words to get off his chest.

"We're a go."

The walls flipped this way and that. He grabbed his garb from its holder and got dressed, staying silent throughout. He noticed Vanessa was ready. She gave him a look. Tugging at different parts of his suit, Markus stopped.

"Something I can do for you, Ms. Vaughn?" he asked.

"A little dust-up with the Missus?" Vanessa cracked.

"I don't see how that concerns you," Markus snapped. "Your business is P4P and the Ivory Fox, I believe. I invite you to keep it that way."

He walked away. She followed him.

"Sorry to break it to you Mr. Doubleday, but you *are* my business," Vanessa told him, a little attitude in her voice. "You may act like you're not, but you'd be wrong."

Markus stopped. So did she. He stoically stared at her. He wasn't used to having more conversation about things after he'd diagnosed them. Stubbornness, he guessed. Without saying another word, Markus slipped his mask on and stepped into his car.

As she walked over to her bike, Vanessa shook her head.

As night fell, the Broken Skull was just getting started. Through his mask, he peered into the mirror.

"Tonight, you will meet your demise," he confidently told himself. "Someone your equal or better awaits. They'll finally put an end to your terrorism. You will fight hard. This night, they will fight harder."

He left the bathroom and made his way to the living area of his makeshift headquarters, where the twins waited.

"We were just starting to worry about you," Emma said.

"Lots of worry," Patrick added.

"No need to worry," the Broken Skull told them. "Everything that's meant to happen will happen … in due time."

"I know this may sound weird, but … we've never seen your face," Patrick mentioned. "I was wondering if we'd ever get to do that. I mean, you see ours all the time. Is it a matter of trust?"

"It's not that," the Broken Skull said. "You chose to do what you will with no mask. I choose to do what I will while masked. After all …"

He took his mask off.

"You never know what people are hiding."

The twins looked on in astonishment. They recognized him immediately.

"Jasper Kane?! I would've never guessed!" Patrick said. "You're on TV all the time, this is just … this is so surreal. I see why you wear a mask."

While Patrick wasted no time shaking Jasper's hand, Emma's skepticism could not be contained. She echoed her brother's sentiments, but she was sure Jasper's disclosure came with a price.

"Because of this trust, my revelation comes with a warning: You're the only two that know my identity. Should someone find me out, I'll assume it was with your assistance. I won't be held responsible for the actions that follow."

The twins understood. Everything would work out fine, as long as they kept each other's identity under wraps. They all understood the ramifications of being loose-lipped.

"With newfound trust brings newfound chemistry," Jasper said. "We will make a push to help people … expand their blinders."

"For The Cause," the group said, one by one.

"The cause of death … looks like another case of you-know-who," Daphne said. She shook her head in disgust. These cases seemed more random than before. The attack was consistent: Blunt force damage without the use of a weapon. Measured injuries. Hand marks around the victim's neck. A fairly clean crime scene.

"There has to be prints somewhere. Let's see what we find," she ordered. The clean-up team got to work while she checked her phone. No calls, no texts. She decided to send a text to Jon.

Another dead one out here. You still want to get in the middle of this?

She hoped he'd say no. The smaller goal was to get a response. She slid her phone into her pocket and surveyed the scene again. A small piece of doubt crept into her mind. Would she be vulnerable again, like the last time the Broken Skull came around?

Her phone's buzz brought her out of her thoughts.

If I know it will help, I won't hesitate.

Wrong answer. She slid her phone back into her pocket and pushed her attention back to the crime scene.

"You're so stupid," Jon said to himself. "So, so stupid."

There was no way he was prepared for what Daphne was talking about. In a text message, anyone could sound like a hero. He paced his apartment.

"If the Broken Skull came in here right now, I'd cry. Without a doubt, I'd cry," he said. Thinking further on it, he shrugged and said, "Well, maybe I'm being dramatic, but it's true. If he kicks my door down, I'm screwed. That's all she wrote. I'm not cut out to wear a mask."

He fell onto the couch and flipped the TV on. He breathed heavily, frustrated. This was his reality.

6

The night went to morning, then to another evening. Marissa wasn't impressed with the finished product of the party's setup, a celebration to launch the P4P Fashion Division. No expense was spared for her new project, whether for elegance or social gatherings.

The days of sloppy-drunk college house parties were gone. In their place was what society viewed as the finer things in life, along with the pomp and circumstance that accompanied the hosting of such things.

Anything that distracted her from Markus's nightly outings was good. She tried to keep her focus away from how long he'd be around on one of the biggest nights of her life.

"That goes there. No, not right there. Okay, back where it was, originally. And … there."

The furniture movers mumbled under their breath with every extra move. Marissa was sure their brains were fried, dealing with her. She was a free spirit at heart, but when it came to how she wanted things to look, "perfectionist" was an understatement.

Markus toured the area. He couldn't help but notice the attention Marissa paid to the party's setup.

"I would ask if you needed help, but it looks like you don't."

"Hey, babe." She moved to peck him on the lips, but stopped herself. She shook her head, as if breaking herself free from her now-embarrassing routine. "Sorry. Anyway, I'm probably going to have them move that again. So I'll see you later on tonight?"

He rubbed his jaw. "Listen, I'm going to try my best."

She shook her head. "Quit being stubborn. It'll look weird if you're late, won't it?" she argued.

"Yes it will. That's why I'm going to keep track of time. I'm the least of your worries, anyway. You have to play the gracious host, and for once, the spotlight isn't on me. I know you're a pro at handling all this, but enjoy it. I'll be back before you know it."

She pointed at him. "And not late?"

"And not late," he repeated. He shrugged one shoulder and said, "Maybe a few minutes."

"Such a comedian," Marissa smiled. He smiled too. She delicately patted his chest with one hand. "I know you want to stay around to support the rearranging of your entire living area."

"Yeah, I can stick around for a bit," he replied. He held the top button on his phone until it shut off. He slid it in his pocket and said, "You have my full attention."

She didn't want to cheapen the experience by accusing him of buttering her up. She knew he genuinely cared. There weren't a lot of people in this entire world that cared like he did. Because of that, she decided to take a chance.

"We're not going to fight about this."

Markus's eyebrows rose. "Fight about what? We're not fighting about anything."

"This whole …" she pointed down to the floor. She was aware and cautious of her surroundings. Now that she knew who The Sound was, security was paramount.

"Would you like to explain what you mean?" Markus questioned.

"Ugh. Listen, all I'm saying is, I don't want to work through any of this. We're already where we need to be, in our relationship."

Markus motioned to the kitchen. "Can we move over here, a little farther away from these people?" Markus suggested. Their voices weren't very loud, but he liked privacy. Their current location made it easy for someone to eavesdrop.

Marissa pulled herself atop the kitchen island. Markus stood across from her, leaning against the kitchen counter.

"So, we're not going to fight about this?" Markus repeated.

"No. I thought about it," Marissa replied.

"What changed your mind?"

"I don't want to be the death of you, with all that nagging. You have a lot of pressure on you, as-is. You run a multi-billion-dollar company and you …" she raised her eyebrows and widened her eyes. While still looking at him, she dropped her head and dramatically nodded.

"I got it," Markus said through a laugh, agreeing with a nod. "Listen, I know I put a lot on your plate, with the …" he half-mockingly showed her what her face looked like. She let a laugh slip, but quickly covered her mouth.

"But seriously … I'm going to try harder, with our relationship. Thank you for understanding the importance of what I do. I appreciate what's between us, even if it seems as though I'm taking it for granted."

Marissa smiled at Markus's good news. "I want to be serious with you for a moment, if I could."

"Sure, go ahead."

"Don't get killed tonight," she said sternly, "or seriously hurt, come to think of it. Don't do any of those things. This night is very important to me, and I'd really like for you to be here."

He started to say something.

"Okay, great!" she interrupted loudly. Her decibel level significantly dropped when she said, "Enjoy your night out, anonymously making the world a better place." Her voice raised back to normal when she said, "Okay, leave me. I have to get this done." She patted him on the chest, pushing him backward on the last tap.

"See you soon." Markus headed through the basement door, slamming it shut. He thought leaving the door cracked for one of the workers to stumble upon his secret was a not-so-original plot. When the platform landed at the bottom, he spoke.

"Computer: The Broken Skull, please."

Holograms of his request popped up, surrounding him as he paced his basement. Lately, he'd become obsessed by the Skull. In the past, he would put his pursuit off for work; now, it bled into his professional life. The eventual meeting between them dominated his thoughts. It was his job to be ready when it happened.

Vanessa was already readying herself in the gym, a room that sat beside the wall that encased their night gear. Equipment that specialized in strength and speed, along with an 80-inch flat screen TV mounted on the wall. The room was for education and "old-fashioned" training.

She was just finishing up her nightly warm-up routine. Perspiration accumulated with every kick and punch. They were slow, but accurate and efficient.

Knock them out. Don't lose control. Fight with ferocity and balance.

"Right," she said to herself.

When she finished, Vanessa draped a towel around her neck and headed to the main area, where she immediately recognized Markus laying waste to large amounts of information. His arms moved so fast while he read. Though she was used to it, Vanessa always found herself impressed by it.

"I'm convinced you're not reading a word of that. I think you do it to look cool."

Markus stopped and zeroed in on Vanessa. She dabbed her face with the towel a few times and returned the gaze. She cracked a weak smile.

"What gave it away?" Markus asked facetiously, starting up his work again.

"I don't know," Vanessa replied. "Maybe I'm jealous because I'll never be able to read that fast."

"Not many can," Markus said matter-of-factly. "Don't worry about it. It's only good if you're in a rush. How was the warm-up?"

"Good-good. Very relaxing. If I can't kick any arse tonight, at least I know I have full range of motion. The consolations in life, I suppose. Are you ready?"

"For what?"

"Ready to go out tonight, of course."

"Oh … yes. I'll follow you out. I'll be trailing by 10, 15 minutes."

"Oh … of course," Vanessa said glumly.

"Trust me, Vanessa. I'm just working overtime on something. I'll be out there before you know it," Markus promised.

"Right. Okay. I'd better get dressed, then."

When Vanessa uttered the words that granted her access to her suit, Markus peered over. He watched her head to the bathroom. When he turned back, his mind was at work.

Trust me, Vanessa. One day, you'll be able to take the reins. You won't care if I'm coming out with you.

In minutes, Vanessa emerged from the bathroom as the Ivory Fox. Markus listened to her approach, followed by the passing of her boots.

"Hey, Vanessa?"

"Yes?"

"I'm proud of what you've done so far."

Vanessa smiled and said, "You've said that before."

She mounted her bike and took off. When Markus heard the garage door close behind her, he stopped working. An exhale escaped. In the past, he couldn't afford a 10 or 15-minute lag.

Vanessa's emergence definitely took some pressure off him, without question.

"Without question, we're making headway on these cases," De La Rosa said. The officers in the meeting room agreed with her words. "The streets have been pretty quiet, except a handful of occasions. We shouldn't take peace lightly. Peace is safety. We'll pay any cost for safety."

An officer raised his hand. De La Rosa acknowledged him with a nod.

"With all due respect, if the streets are quiet … can't we just leave it be?" he asked. "The Sound and all these masks … can't we just let it go?"

"Well, I'm glad we asked you," De La Rosa said. The room erupted in laughter. "We can wait if you want, but it's eventually going to happen. We can take our time and do it slow, or we can sweep the streets quick, wipe out every target on our list. Besides, you mind telling me why you want to wait?"

The officer cleared his throat.

"I just wanna make sure we're doing this the right way. No disrespect."

"Raise your hand if you've done this before." Daphne raised her hand and looked around the room. No one else raised theirs. "Oh … just checking. Well, maybe you should sit back and listen, then?"

The officer was caught off-guard by the way Daphne talked to him.

"Not that you deserve an explanation, but I don't want to wait because I'm tired of it going on," Daphne said. "People need to remember, we're the law. You want to send a message? This is the best way to do it."

She thought back to her time as a young officer, assisting in a similar project. She'd made a few arrests, but some officers took it a step further. That left a brutal - but effective - impression.

She remembered the plan of attack: Masks were so wrapped up in their own agendas, they wouldn't see the pick-off coming. The years passed, but the same self-serving motives remained.

"I expect everyone in this room to get down for this cause. Is everyone in agreement?"

Daphne examined the room again. The gathered agreed with their eyes and their heads. No words were spoken, just a rock-solid understanding within the congregation.

Except one. Daphne noticed the defector almost instantly.

"You got a problem with the way we're handling this?" Daphne asked, an aggressive tone clinging to every word.

"I don't have a problem with the way it's being handled," the officer said. "I have a problem with *who* is handling it."

He stood up and shuffled through the row of officers into the narrow aisle. Daphne met him in the middle. She looked him in the eye.

"Oh, you need a man in charge?" she questioned, sarcasm laced in every word. "Will that make the streets safer?"

Miffed, the officer refrained from making eye contact with her. Her eyes remained on him. Her fists clenched, she took a step forward, now inches from him.

"I got news for you: Whatever savior-with-a-dick you're hoping for, they're not coming. You understand?" she asked the officer.

He didn't respond.

"I said … do you … understand?!" she repeated. This time, her jaw was clenched. Her knuckles were well on their way to turning white.

"Yes, ma'am," was all the officer said.

"You're a part of this now, whether you like it or not." She pointed toward the seat he previously vacated. "Sit down."

Annoyed, the officer pushed his way through the sea of legs and parked himself back in his seat. De La Rosa returned to the front of the room and scanned all the eyes on her. She looked specifically for the officer she just had a run-in with. He hadn't blinked. She liked that.

"Are there anymore questions about who's in charge?" she asked.

The room was silent.

"That's what I thought. Dismissed."

As the officers filed out of the meeting room, Daphne eyed every last one of them. She wouldn't tolerate another officer stepping out of line, she couldn't afford it. Now, they knew that.

On the other side of town, the Starks twins and the Broken Skull devised a plan to meet with The Sound, the Ivory Fox, or both.

As always, Patrick voted for the "Smash and Grab" technique – make trouble and hope it was enough to draw enemies out. Emma and the Broken Skull were more tactful and conniving than Patrick's ill-advised strategy.

A blueprint was constructed to draw the heroes out. One thing Emma respected about the Broken Skull, he did his homework. He was quick with probabilities, ways to quantify a target's whereabouts. They'd go where the Ivory Fox and The Sound frequented most, according to what the hands on their watches read.

In an alleyway, the three sat in the back of their van.

"Maybe we can do my thing tonight?" Patrick asked.

"Oh, you *would* like your song played tonight, wouldn't you?" Emma teased.

"Stop it," Patrick smiled. "Seriously, wouldn't it be easier to beat up some random? Draw them out that way?"

"Perhaps," the Broken Skull said. "There are two sides to every coin. I love violence as much as the next, but some things come easier without it. This would be one of those times."

"But … fun!" Patrick pleaded. "Okay, if you say so. You're the boss."

"I'm not the boss. We all work together, remember?" the Skull corrected.

"I'm sure he apologizes," Emma said, much to Patrick's dismay. He didn't understand where Emma's words came from, but he wouldn't comment further.

While the Broken Skull explained his plan, he heard the sound of a motorcycle. His head shot up. He placed his hand on the van's door handle and checked his watch.

"Right on time," the Broken Skull said. "My calculations were correct."

Patrick and Emma looked at each other and smirked, impressed. To know exactly where she would be, at that exact time was remarkable.

Without warning, the Broken Skull shoved the van's side door open and extended his arm. First, the screeching of tires. Then, the sounds of a crash.

The three approached the Fox as she writhed in the alleyway. Pain was spread across her face as she forced herself up to all fours. She shook her head and looked around. The three didn't know what she was looking for. As they stood above her, she looked up.

"Won't hurt a bit," Patrick said.

He bunched up a handful of her hair and clamped down. While she struggled with his grip, he stuck a small syringe in the side of her neck and pushed the plunger down until all the liquid disappeared. The Fox's eyes widened. His grip loosened. She crawled away from them, struggling with every movement. Seconds later, she was motionless.

"Get some restraints, please. We will need them," the Broken Skull ordered. The twins nodded and returned to the van. Soon after, they came back with a few strands of rope and tied the Fox up, the two carrying her limp body back to the van. With Patrick at the wheel, the van pulled off into the night.

7

Back at the Doubleday estate, the house quickly became a sea of partygoers and potential customers. Conversations were alive with speculation as to what the Doubleday/Buchanan union had to offer. Critics were there to critique, others were there to ogle, and the rest were there to be jealous. Marissa didn't get nervous much in these situations, but right before show time, she always felt a pang.

"I'm glad I didn't eat Thai food," she muttered to herself.

She cruised through the crowd like a pro, air-kissing, light-hugging, and well-wishing. Ever the generous extrovert, Marissa made friends at funerals. Still, thoughts floated around in her mind.

Markus better be on his way back. Ahgod, I'm second-guessing myself about letting him go! He's going to get killed! It'll ruin this whole thing, I just know it!

She ran her hands over her outfit and inhaled.

Stop being so morbid, Marissa! You know you can't hide when you think something's gross! Don't turn your nose up! Just settle down. Everything's going to be just fine.

Marissa snapped out of her thoughts when a microphone was pushed in her face. She saw Titus passing by, so she snaked an arm around his.

"You all right?" Titus asked her, taken aback by the sudden yank.

"Yeah, just hold my hand while I talk to these people," she answered.

Titus nodded. Marissa exhaled and lightly patted it a few times. People turned toward the noise when they heard it. She grinned out of the corner of her mouth and brought the microphone near her lips.

She asked the crowd, "Are we good? This is on, right?"

The crowd loudly let her know they could hear her. She beamed at the response she got from the house's inhabitants.

"So … welcome to the P4P Fashion Launch!" Marissa exclaimed. "For you Nosey Nancy's, Markus is running a little late. Yes, I know it's his house and yes, he knows I'm throwing a big ol' party in it."

The group let out a collective laugh at Marissa's words. She continued.

"Let me start off by thanking my fabulous designer, Titus. Without him, this dream would still be a dream. He's the real brains behind this operation. Thank you, Titus."

The assembled crowd clapped, mostly together. Titus gave a small, sarcastic wave to the crowd, raising his eyebrows along with his hand motion.

"To be honest, tonight's not about Markus, Titus, or even me. It's about providing a product that people enjoy. However … if my name's on it, you know what you're getting. P4P won't accept second. Never have, never will."

The crowd clapped. Marissa nodded her head in agreement.

"Second of all, we're going to have a good time tonight. Don't forget to take the goody bag on your way out. Attendants will be around to take care of your drinks and answer questions about what Titus and I have cooked up for you. With that being said, here's to fun!"

The audience saluted her efforts with a raise of their glasses. One wave from her, and the music resumed. She turned the microphone off and tossed it back to the DJ. She turned back to Titus.

"All right. How was that?" she asked him.

"All of it was good!" he said. "You make it look so easy. It certainly helps that everyone loves you!"

She smiled at his words.

"Not that I need to mention, but you look fabulous," a well-dressed Titus told her. The two kissed each other's cheeks. "Say, did you have help designing that dress?"

"As if I have to say," she replied. "Have I thanked you lately for making this move with me?

"One more couldn't hurt," he joked. Or, Marissa thought he was joking. "So, you need to dish: Where's Marky-Mark? No Funky Bunch, either?" he asked.

"Ah, another pet name for Markus. Well, you know how he is: success before rest. Vanessa … is also not here."

She wished she could tell Titus where Markus really was. She wanted one person to share with. Just one. In reality, she had no way of knowing his location. She remembered the night she tried tracking him. He was everywhere and nowhere, at the same time. It was baffling.

"He better show up," Titus warned. "I'm not going to do anything, but he better show. Just because he's handsome ... and barrel-chested ... and muscular ... and kind ... that don't mean he can fight."

Titus' cautioning was followed by a hearty laugh from Marissa. *You don't know the half of it*, she thought. "Oh, stop. You don't want to fight him; you want to hug him," Marissa said confidently.

"You know me like the back of your hand. Do you think he might have time for a hug, if he shows up?" Titus wondered.

"*When*, Titus. *When* he shows up."

"Uh-huh. When he shows up. Sorry."

Marissa waved off his half-hearted apology. "Don't you have a date, or something?"

"Oh, he's around here somewhere." Titus barely scanned the room and looked back at Marissa. He was more enamored with the glitz and the glamour, the pageantry of Marissa's launch. It also furthered his career, something he cared very much about.

One of the things Marissa always liked about Titus: He had enough ambition to know he wouldn't be her assistant forever.

Deep down, she wondered if Markus felt that way about Vanessa.

The van turning one way and the other woke Vanessa out of her forced slumber. She groggily batted her eyes a few times. It was dark. The van felt rickety. The van bounced more than a normal vehicle; bad suspension, she thought. She shook her head and squinted. One in the driver seat, one in the passenger seat. She felt like she was on nighttime medicine.

"It's good that you're up," she heard. She moved around, but not much. While gaining her surroundings, she realized she was hog-tied. She sighed to herself. This definitely wasn't the way she saw her night going.

Then she saw him. The Broken Skull.

She'd never been that close before, only pictures. He sat against one of the walls of the van, knees pulled up, legs split open, hands on his knees. She listened to his breathing pattern. Periodically, he would turn his head. She swore he was staring at her. She decided against speaking. Defending herself was impossible.

After a few minutes, the van slowed to a stop. The two in the front disappeared, reappearing to open the side door. They drug Vanessa out by her arms. Her knees dragged across the dirt, the weight providing extra pressure for sharp rocks to poke through. She felt the rocks break her skin and settle in her knees.

Vanessa's words came out slow when she said, "You've got to do something about this road."

"Shut up," Patrick said.

"No way to treat our guest," the Broken Skull said. "Perhaps she could be persuaded to stay longer if we were a little more accommodating."

"I won't be staying long," she said.

No one acknowledged her words, just kept dragging her along. She heard a door unlocked and opened. They dragged her a few more feet, then dropped her. The side of her head hit the cold surface. She crinkled her nose and gnashed her teeth. She ran her tongue along her bottom lip. She tasted blood, a taste she hated. Ever since Markus told her about how he knew he made a mistake, Vanessa couldn't look at it any other way.

She tasted her own blood. She was bound and barely awake. She did something wrong.

Markus cruised along as The Sound. As he navigated the streets, he wondered what time he'd get back to his house for Marissa's launch. He hated to cut a night short, but he agreed to it. Breaking appointments wasn't his style.

"I wonder what Vanessa is up to."

He pushed a few buttons on his steering wheel and waited. Moments later, holograms showed her bike's whereabouts. He was headed the wrong way. He turned the car around and headed in that direction.

In minutes, Markus arrived in the alleyway. He looked down the alley through his windshield. He noticed Vanessa's bike, lying on its side. He got out of the car and walked down the grimy alley, looking for any clues.

Nothing.

When he made it to Vanessa's bike, he crouched down and examined it. His first thought was usually the worst case scenario.

She skidded, from the way the tires look. She was forced off her bike. Abduction. But where?

Markus picked up Vanessa's bike and punched a few buttons. "Go home," he commanded. The bike revved up and took off down the alley. When Markus returned back to his car, he manually looked up Vanessa's whereabouts.

Where could she be?

Vanessa had no idea where she was. Her captors did a good job of keeping her surroundings dark, starting with the van ride. She wondered how much experience they had with this. The one thing she noticed on her way in was the long dirt road leading to the house. A little more than a minute, at average speed. She figured it was a mile or so.

Now sitting in a single chair in the living area of the empty dwelling, Vanessa moved her appendages. Her wrists were tied tight behind the chair. She tried moving her legs. They were tied together. She looked down. They'd tied her up across her chest.

"Must not want me to go anywhere," Vanessa said. "Well, now that it's established that I have nowhere to go …"

"You sure do have a smart mouth," Patrick said.

Emma said, "She can talk all she wants. No matter what she says, she's all tied up."

"Nobody wants to talk to the help. You two are clearly the help," Vanessa said. "Where'd the *real* brains of the operation go?"

Emma burned on the inside from her hostage's words. She hated being referred to as "the help." She knew Patrick hated it, too. Instead of losing her composure, Emma kept her voice playful.

"Oh, he's cooking up something for you," Emma told her. "And when he's done, you'll be right where we want you. You'll get what's coming to you. We all do, in the end."

"You're probably safer here than you are out in the street," Patrick said.

"Of course she is," Emma added.

"You have the cops shooting at you, among other things," he said.

"And … don't you usually patrol the streets with someone else?" she asked Vanessa.

"I think you know the answer to that," Vanessa said. "If I were you, whatever you're going to do, make it quick. It's only a matter of time before he finds me, and when he does … you're in big, big trouble."

"Trouble has its way of finding me … but I love the company."

Vanessa turned toward the voice. The Broken Skull slowly approached from the hallway, holding a small, metallic tray. Now standing by his accomplices, the twins grinned.

Vanessa subtly wriggled her wrist, banged it up against the chair. Nothing.

"There is no escape," the Broken Skull said. "I trust my cohorts with something as simple as tying someone up. You'll find your struggle ultimately ... fruitless."

Vanessa glared at him. Seeing him on TV was one thing, but to see him this close up was altogether different. She understood why so many feared him. His get-up and his physical size proved imposing.

"The Ivory Fox ... what a great get," the Broken Skull said to his family members. "My greatest capture will be your running mate. To draw him out, I need some kind of ... equalizer."

He pulled a syringe off the tray Emma now held. He just barely pushed the plunger down, watching some of the liquid squirt out. He nodded yes and started his approach toward the Fox.

Patrick lunged and grabbed her head. One hand gripped her forehead and the other hand grabbed her chin to force her head up. She tried to move her head around, but stopped when she felt Patrick's grip tighten. She winced when she felt his fingernails dig into her skin.

"The great ... equalizer," the Skull said. He plunged the needle into the Fox's neck. She let out a yelp when she felt the needle's pinch. She grimaced as he pushed the plunger down. She felt the foreign substance already working into her system. Her eyes got heavy. Within seconds, her head sunk.

The Ivory Fox was out.

8

"Are you awake?"

"I am."

"Do you know where you are?"

"No, can't say that I do."

"Who am I speaking with?"

"The Ivory Fox."

She looked refreshed, blinked deep a few times. She felt like she'd gotten a night's sleep. She looked around. The same three surrounded her.

"I'm going to ask you some questions. Can you answer them for me?" the Broken Skull asked.

"I believe I can," Ivory Fox replied. She felt the liquid coursing through her veins. It made her feel loose, like she wasn't in complete control. She knew she shouldn't talk to these people, but it became harder as time passed. She winced again.

My head's killing me. It had to be that shot. What was that?

"Let's start simple: Who do you work with?" the Skull asked.

"The Sound," she replied.

"And what do you do?" he asked.

"We fight crime at night, make sure the streets stay safe."

"You've done a commendable job."

"Thank you."

"What do you do in the daytime?" he asked.

Vanessa blinked hard a few times and bit her lip. Her head started to pound, increasingly getting worse. Then, it started to burn. She felt her brain searing inside her head. Her body tensed up. She stomped the ground repeatedly. Her abdominal muscles crunched.

"I work … just like anybody … else!" she barely managed to get out.

The Broken Skull nodded. "I'll be patient. You'll tell me everything. They always do. You'll tell me everything, and we can get on with our plans. Next question: Do you really think you can defeat us?"

Without hesitation, Vanessa said, "Yes."

"And what are your plans for that?"

Another burning wave of discomfort. She closed her eyes. Her toes curled. Her knees banged together. She dipped her head low and bit her lip again. This time, she drew blood. She tried focusing on the pain. The more she fought, the more pain it brought.

She just wanted the burning to stop.

Vanessa's shoulders hunched. One of her eyes welled up. It gathered and dripped, like a slow-leaking faucet. A couple even ran out of her eye and onto her cheek before breaking off and hitting her thigh.

"We plan on stopping you! We *will* stop you!" she screamed.

"Who is The Sound?" the Broken Skull screamed, matching her intensity.

Her mouth got tight as she shook her head no. Her nostrils flared. She closed her eyes again. Her neck muscles tightened up. Her fingers expanded and contracted. Her mouth opened, but nothing came out. She looked up to the ceiling of the house as tears streamed down her face.

"Tell me," the Broken Skull said. "Let it out."

"I will not!" she screamed. She looked at him before dropping her head again.

While Vanessa's cries echoed throughout the house, Emma grabbed Patrick's forearm and squeezed. Patrick looked down at his sister. She silently implored him to say something. He shook her off. He knew better than to question the Broken Skull while he worked. With his eyes, he made sure Emma knew not to, as well.

Vanessa's cries stopped, replaced by delirious laughter. Her head slowly perked up. She let out an energetic giggle.

"Who is he?!" the Broken Skull's voice raised.

"He's …" Vanessa stuttered.

"He's …" the Broken Skull prompted. He leaned in and nodded his head in anticipation.

"He's … going to kick your ass so bad," she said through laughter. She raised her eyebrows. "You're going to hate it. Just you wait, you."

With the speed of a gun's hammer hitting the barrel, Vanessa reared back and head-butted the Broken Skull, catching him on the bridge of his nose.

Vanessa loaded all the pressure on her feet and jumped back, breaking the chair into pieces when she landed. She rolled backward. Patrick pulled a knife and lunged at her. Vanessa's body bent forward, dodging the knife. She shot her arms up, using the knife to cut the binding in half. He swiped at her again. She fell to her back. Patrick sliced downward. Vanessa raised her legs and straightened them out, letting him cut the binding from her legs. She kicked him in the side of the knee as hard as she could, buckling him. She flipped to her feet and hit him thrice, dropping him.

The Broken Skull recovered and gathered speed. Vanessa turned toward him and jumped, hitting him in the chest with a vicious front drop kick. The force staggered him, but he quickly caught himself.

Everyone froze. Vanessa stared down her captors. Their collective gazes clung to her. Breathing filled the small living area.

Run.

Adrenaline overtook whatever the Skull injected her with. Fire in her eyes, she turned and ran, diving through one of the glass windows like a missile. One somersault later and she was off. Her legs churned down the dirt road with urgency. Nothing mattered more than escape. While she kept her sprint up, she hit a couple buttons on her wrist.

"I'm already en route, just turning the corner," she heard Markus say.

Vanessa yelled exhaustedly into her wrist receiver. "I'm on foot and headed your way!" She heard the van start up in the far distance. She picked up her speed with what she had left. She didn't know how much longer she could keep her pace up. Her legs were on fire. She felt herself getting winded.

Vanessa saw headlights in front of her, moving at an uncomfortable speed.

"When I say jump, jump," she heard through her wrist receiver. She couldn't afford any mistakes, now that the van was gaining on her. The van would be on her heels in 20 seconds or less, she guessed.

Markus's car closed in.

"Jump!" she heard.

She concentrated all her energy into her legs and exploded off the ground. Markus's car skidded forward and whipped around. Her legs clipped the back of the car. She rolled from one side to the other, catching herself at the last second, clutching the inside of the roof of the car. Her fingers dug into the interior as the car jerked forward and picked up speed again.

Vanessa looked in the rear view mirror. The van was approaching too fast. "Brace for impact!" Vanessa yelled into the car. The front of the van slammed into the back of Markus's car, pushing it forward. It fishtailed one way, then the other, then picked up speed again.

"Hold on!" Markus told Vanessa.

"What other choice do I have?!" she yelled back at him.

The van picked up speed. So did Markus's car. The car jerked forward again, this time, leaving the van in the dust. The damaged front end and headlights faded into the darkness. Vanessa tightened her grip in anticipation of another turn. When Markus hit the sharp turn, he yelled to Vanessa, "Slide in through the passenger window! No time to stop!"

Vanessa did as she was told, folding her body through the window opening and settling into the passenger's seat. When she latched on her safety belt, Markus punched the gas, his car exploding down the street. He punched a few buttons on his dashboard screen and made a few turns.

"Oh my God," Vanessa said. "I could've stuck myself to the roof of your car and didn't. That was way harder than need be."

"Just rest up. We're going home," Markus told her. "I'm sorry. I should've gone out with you. I'm sorry this happened to you."

"No need to apologize," Vanessa told him, her voice a little higher than a whisper. "I'm just going to get my heart out of my throat real quick."

Some minutes later, the garage door opened. His car shot down the ramp and then slowed into the designated parking space. Markus unlatched his safety belt and pushed himself out of the car, circling around to the other side. He scooped Vanessa up and carried her with a fast-paced walk.

"I need a Recovery Chamber for Vanessa Vaughn, please," Markus said.

A horizontal chamber rose from the floor. The door to it unlatched and slowly opened. He laid Vanessa inside the chamber, unzipping and peeling the snugly-fit suit off her, along with her boots. He pulled her mask off and looked at her. She looked at him. He noticed her skin raised on the side of her neck.

"Did they shoot you with something?" Markus asked.

"Yeah, some kind of something, I don't know," Vanessa responded. "It made me want to tell the truth."

"I'm sure it's still in you, whatever it is."

"Markus … am I going to die?" she asked him.

"I don't know," Markus answered. "I don't know what they injected you with. Just rest. You've never been *this* banged up. The chamber's going to pull the glass out of your face. It's also going to pull the toxins from your blood. It's going to be a painful process, but it's going to fix you. Let it do the job. I'll be right upstairs. I'll come down as soon as the party is over, I promise."

While the door to the Recovery Chamber slowly lowered, it occurred to Markus that he had to move his hand. He slowly unhanded her, the last couple fingertips running across each other before the chamber door shut.

She'll be all right.

Markus stepped into the elevator that sat just past his suit inventory. Though he didn't have time to get in the party mood, the gentle ascension calmed him. He didn't have much time to undress, so he took his mask off and dressed up in one of the suits handed to him by a descending hanger. Once he got dressed, he felt around for discrepancies.

Markus descended from the top of the stairs. While doing so, he got the feel of his surroundings as he scanned the room for Marissa.

There she is.

He made his way over to her. She was talking to some people he'd met before, but couldn't place. His mind was everywhere else but at the party. He needed to adjust to his surroundings.

"Excuse me," Marissa politely said to her company. She checked her watch and looked at him. He shrugged. She took the necessary few steps to meet him. They traded cheek kisses before she tugged at the collar of his suit and leaned in his ear.

"Did you not take off your Sound suit?" she asked him.

"No," he whispered back, "just the mask. I was running late, and I told you I wouldn't be late. I was going as fast as I could."

"It's showing."

Markus moved to fiddle with his collar.

"No. Stop. I'm already doing that," she reminded him. "Is everything okay? You look a little off."

"Yeah, I just … mental lapse. I'm sorry. Is everything good? Do you need anything right now?"

"We'll talk later. It looks like you need to collect yourself," Marissa said. "I'm worried about you, so you need to find a bathroom, get everything right and good, and I'll meet you back out here, okay?"

"Okay."

"Okay, good."

She kissed him on the jaw and walked away. He adjusted the lapels of his suit jacket and strode to the nearest bathroom. He shut the door and locked it, looked in the mirror.

"What the hell is going on?" he whispered to himself. He looked at where he slipped up. He couldn't believe it. The normally detail-oriented billionaire found himself upset at the mistake he made. He shook his head and looked himself over again. He made a mental note to get a laundry chute installed, just in case. His phone buzzed.

You and I have business to discuss. I'll come to you.

Markus sent a quick one back.

You know your daughter is hosting a party here right?

His phone buzzed again, as soon as he tried to pocket it.

What I have going on is more important. See you in 15.

Markus looked at the ceiling, blew the air out of his lungs and closed his eyes. It felt like one thing after another was happening. Very rarely did he ever come straight from the field to something as big as a product launch. All he wanted to do was be by Vanessa's side. Everything else seemed so unimportant.

Markus took a few deep breaths and looked himself over again.

All good.

Within seconds, he was shaking hands and fraternizing with guests. He wasn't hosting, but he represented Marissa. Impressions were still important. He never underestimated the power of professional relationships. Being nice was a good rule of thumb.

Deciding to put those thoughts on the backburner, Markus worked through the crowd until he reunited with Marissa.

"Okay. I'm good," he told her.

Marissa gave him a quick once-over and said, "You look better. Much better."

Markus felt a tap on his shoulder. He barely turned, at first. When he saw who it was, he turned around completely.

"Mr. Buchanan. I didn't see you come in. Sorry about that."

"Just missed your speech, regrettably," Michael said. He kissed his only daughter on the cheek. "Sorry, Honey. Hey Markus … a word?"

"Yeah. Not a problem, Mr. Buchanan." He looked at Marissa.

Michael led the way. Markus counted two that followed.

"You know what this is about?" Markus asked.

"Not a clue," Marissa said. "I'm actually surprised to see him. Totally unexpected."

He sensed nervousness from her.

"Okay. Listen, go have fun," he said lightheartedly. "This is your night. I'm going to go talk shop with your dad for a few. Be right back."

"No. I want to go with you," Marissa demanded.

He immediately shook his head no at the idea.

"I don't think it's that big a deal. I'll be back before you know it. Even though this is my house, you're actually hosting this thing. I don't want you to risk looking antisocial."

"Just know that I'm only staying back because you make a great point," Marissa said. "But I want a nightcap later, so don't even think about going anywhere else, got it?" she asked.

"Loud and clear," he said. "Go have fun."

Markus left her side. As he walked through the crowd and blankly acknowledged people, he wondered why Michael showed up. What did he want? His wheels turned and turned, still turning when he finally made it outside. To stop himself from overthinking the situation more, he distracted himself with words.

"Mr. Buchanan."

"Markus Doubleday, the great and powerful," Michael said. "You know why I'm here?"

Markus shook his head no. He'd already sized up the two that followed Michael. He was no longer focused on why Michael was there. Instead, he focused on the possibility of chaos breaking out, mid-conversation. He stayed just outside of arm's reach from the three.

"I'm here because of something a little birdie told me," Michael said. "Now, it may've slipped your mind because it's been a few months, but there was a matter with Dwight Durant and my daughter. Remember that night?"

"Yeah."

"You ran."

Markus hesitated. It was already escalating out of his control. Reacting any faster would put him in hot water. He wanted to tell Michael he didn't run. Instead, he made the tough decision to fall on his own sword. He inhaled and exhaled through his nostrils and crossed his arms.

"You ran, and you didn't even have the decency to take Marissa with you, you coward. What the hell is the matter with you? Were you that scared?" he asked.

"I'm sorry Mr. Buchanan," Markus said.

"Oh, you're sorry? Damn right, you're sorry!" Michael told him. "Listen to me …"

He grabbed Markus by the lapels of his jacket, pulled him in close. He shook his head no and said, "I don't care how in love she thinks she is with you, understand?" he asked. Markus moved his head away slightly. Looking past Michael, he saw Michael's help tense up, ready to make a move at any moment.

"If you ever … *ever* run again, with my daughter in danger … you better keep running. Out of the city, the state, even this country. Do you understand?!"

"Okay … okay, I get it," Markus said. He placed his hands up just above his shoulders. "I didn't mean to, I just … panicked. It was a total slip-up, Michael. It'll never happen aga–"

"Shut up."

Michael dug his knuckles into Markus's chest before shoving him. He then walked back into the house, followed by his cronies. The last one purposely bumped Markus as he passed. While Markus smoothed over his wrinkled lapels, he looked up at the night sky.

Keeping up this soft, non-confrontational appearance definitely has its drawbacks, especially when it would take less than 10 seconds to dismantle them.

He smiled.

Fifteen, at the most.

After hours of playing gracious host, it was time to say goodbye to the partygoers. A Buchanan party was essentially a Doubleday party: one hell of a party (with a hard stopping time).

Markus loosened up his tie and pulled it over his head, laying it to rest on the kitchen island. After unbuttoning the top buttons of his dress shirt, he pulled out the two glasses he'd warmed up and poured some drinks: A Manhattan for her, a Scotch and soda for him. When Marissa arrived, Markus handed her the glass.

She exhaled. "Great night, right?" she asked him, excitement slathered on her face.

"Yeah, great night," Markus said.

"So we can toast to success, you know, since we're resting now," she notified.

Markus held his glass up to hers and barely clanked it, then took his drink down in one gulp.

"What's wrong?" she wondered. "What did my dad say to you?"

"Nothing big. Just talked business."

"Is this about the restaurant thing? The thing with Dwight?"

"Just business."

"But you don't have any business with my father, Markus. Stop saying it's just business."

"He thinks I ran. I didn't run, but what was I going to do? Tell him?"

Marissa took a sip of her drink. "That's the way it looked, though."

Markus clearly bristled at her words. He poured another drink.

"Listen … if you broke down and told him you were The Sound, I'd support you. If you decided to let him think you ran, then I support that, too. Are you getting my drift, here?"

"Yeah," he said, downing another Scotch and soda.

"Your smile looks like the hundreds I saw tonight. Markus … what did he say to you?"

"He told me if I ran out on you like that again, he'd basically kill me," Markus said.

"He really said that?"

"Yeah. I believed him."

Marissa cocked her head forward. "Why would you believe something like that?"

"Because he killed Dwight."

Marissa blinked at Markus's words, turning her head toward him skeptically. "Wha- … What? How do you know that? He didn't do that. He'd never do that. Where are you getting your information from?" she pressed.

"It doesn't matter where I got it from. I have it. You can tell me your dad's a good guy until you're blue in the face, but deep down, you know better. We know better."

"That's a very rude thing to say," Marissa commented.

"I didn't think I had to mince words with you. Words shouldn't tear us apart."

She crossed her arms and hunched her shoulders slightly. She blinked a few times.

"You being The Sound would tear us apart before anything my dad did would," she said. "I didn't want a nightcap with you so we could play the Blame Game. Up until a few months ago, I thought you wanted more in life than to destroy yourself every night, worrying about a problem that's never going to go away. So … should we drink to that? Self-destruction?"

She held her drink up.

"We're done here." Markus snatched his tie off the kitchen island and walked away. He could argue all night with her, but it wouldn't help anything. He stood to lose a lot more, if he did that.

Across town, there was a light scratch at the door that brought Jonathan out of his slumber. With one eye open, his sight veered over to the clock on the nightstand. Two a.m.

"What the heck?" he asked himself. Cats had started coming around recently, and it drove him crazy.

Maybe if I stop feeding them, they'll stop coming around.

"Must be mating season," he said to himself, kicking the covers off his body and stepping out of his still-floored bed. He rubbed his face, and then rubbed his eyes with his knuckled-up hands. After a few steps, he'd gained full balance.

When he arrived at the door, he sweetly said, "Get out of here, kitty. I'm trying to sleep." As he walked away, he muttered, "Just like everybody else."

Another knock.

"Ugh! Come on!" he said frustratedly. He opened the door.

He immediately shut it.

"Wait! Wait!" he heard through the door. A single arm flailed, pinned against the door frame.

"If you don't move your arm, I'm going to slam it again!" Jon threatened, his back steady against the door.

"I'm alone! I swear! Please!" the voice said. "I'm not moving my arm, so if you want to slam it, then slam it!"

Jon thought about it for a moment before he relented. He let off a bit, enough for the girl to slip her arm out. He turned around and kept his curled toes against the door.

"What do you want?" Jon asked, one eye fixed on her while she stood in the hallway.

"I just … I wanted to apologize for what happened," she said. "Can you open the door? I'm at your mercy, here. I promise there's no one with me. I know I lied to you before, but just give me five seconds."

Jon closed his eyes for a second, long enough to curse his soft heart.

"It's open," he said.

"Okay, thank you," she said. She pushed the door open and walked in. When she shut it, she rested against the door and held her elbow. Jon grabbed his phone off the counter, punched a few numbers and held the phone in his hand.

"Before this continues, just know that I've dialed 911 into my phone. All I have to do is push Send."

"That's fair," she said.

"Now, what is your *real* name?" Jon asked.

"It's really Emma. Emma Starks. And that was really my brother, Patrick."

"So, what kind of setup is this?"

"There isn't one. I'm serious. He doesn't even know I'm here. Nobody does."

"So, you just came to apologize? I don't get it. It's been months."

"I'm apologizing because … I want a shot at a new life. I've never killed anyone, but I've been present for some grisly things. When I met you, you came across as someone genuine, real. You were just … normal. I want normal."

"I don't know what any of this has to do with me, but I'm sorry I hurt your arm."

"I'll consider us even," Emma said. "I wanted to ask you something."

"This is it, so make it good," Jon said. "Honestly, I don't feel the most comfortable, alone with you. I hope you understand."

"Well, that's kind of what I wanted to ask. Would you feel more comfortable in a public place?"

"A public place would've been better, yes."

Jon noticed Emma's eyes sparkle in the shallow darkness of his phone. Jon never bothered to turn the lights on while they talked.

"Okay, so I'll see you for breakfast?" Emma said.

Jon was confused. "What?"

"Sounds perfect. Meet me at the Crooked Tree at 8 a.m."

All Jon could do was watch as she left out the door. He didn't wait for her to get down the hallway. He slammed the door shut and locked it, the deadbolt and the chain, too. He wasn't taking any chances.

"What the heck did I just agree to?" he asked himself. "Did I even agree to it? The Crooked Tree at 8? What if her brother is there? He wouldn't beat me up in a public place, would he?" he questioned as he walked back to his room. He rummaged around his closet until he found what he was looking for. "She's gotta be crazy. I think she's crazy."

He lay back down in his bed, holding his baseball bat close.

Speaking of close, Jasper Kane hadn't heard from his girlfriend in hours. He'd driven by her place. All the lights were off. It wasn't like her to ignore her phone, even when sleeping. He'd called numerous times. No answer. In his house, he paced.

His tone was quiet when he said, "I shouldn't be feeling this way, with the line of work I'm in. I'm worried. I don't have time to feel this way. I'm not ... emotionally stable enough to feel this way."

His pacing kept up. Patrick and Emma were gone. The Broken Skull had been put to rest for the night. This night brought a different feeling. Was it worse because he wasn't able to finish off the Ivory Fox?

"Better to sleep on it," he diagnosed. He sat on his couch, in the darkness, tilting his head back on the back of his couch.

9

Morning came.

Jon didn't know how long he'd dozed off. He relaxed his hands and let go of the bat. He'd held it close all night, like a loved one. He pushed out of bed and ran his fingers through his hair, detangling his mane.

He looked in the bathroom mirror. "You're not seriously thinking of going to meet her, are you?" he asked himself, attempting to rub his eyes free of the redness. "She's insane. I mean, *certified* insane. I really think if I show up …"

Jon ran both hands along the sides of his face, up and down.

"What else do I have going on?" Jon asked himself before he stepped in the shower. The hot water hit his body, waking him almost immediately, but also soothing him. He rested his head underneath the shower head and let the water run.

"Is it me, or does it seem like I only attract the crazy ones?" he asked himself as he scrubbed. "I mean, De La Rosa is probably crazy, right? And listen, don't get me started on this Emma Starks. All I want in my life is for someone not to threaten or attempt to kill me. Is it really too much to ask?"

He looked up. No answer.

"Of course. Well, at least I'm clean."

After getting dressed and out of the house, he drove to the Crooked Tree. When he parked, he looked at the time on his dashboard. Almost 8. Instead of waiting at the door for her, Jon sat himself and perused the menu.

Within minutes, Emma walked through the shop's doors. Jon noticed Emma's eyes scanning the place. He raised his hand and gave her half a wave. As she approached, Jon wiped his hands on his jeans.

"Is something on you?" he heard. He stopped.

"No … well, kind of," he said quickly. "How are you?"

Emma took a seat across from him.

"Oh, I'm good," she said. "Yourself?"

"Still a little on edge, I'm afraid," he admitted.

"Which reminds me: Oh, Patrick?" she said loudly.

"Sh–"

Jon shifted out of his chair quickly, looking around for Patrick. Emma grabbed his wrist. They looked at each other. While he lightly scanned the room - and caught every eye on them because of Emma's outburst - he felt her hand around his wrist relax, and then move down to his hand.

"Patrick's not here," she told him innocently. "I told you he wouldn't be around."

"You can see where I *wouldn't* believe that, right?" he asked.

She nodded yes and slowly let his hand go. He sat back down.

"Everything has to be out on the table," Jon proclaimed.

She barely shrugged. "I'm an open book. Let me know what you want to know, and I'll try my best to answer."

Emma was dangerous. He felt it in her touch. He imagined how many guys had fallen in love with that caress. He also imagined how many guys had been burned by it.

"Do you want me to believe that you just want to be normal?" Jon asked. "You said it yourself, you've been a part of some grisly things. That doesn't just go away because you want it to."

"I agree with you. It doesn't. That doesn't mean I'm going to stop trying," Emma responded. "I know my brother punching your lights out is a hard thing to get past."

Jon subtly threw his hands up and huffed. "Yeah, it totally is. You know, because he punched me. Like, knocked me out cold, for no real reason."

"Yeah, I had a front-row seat. Anyway, if you don't want to try to be friends, that's completely fine."

"I'm here, so that counts for something, right?"

"Yes, it does. So, if I remember correctly, you had a thing for a certain detective. Care to share?"

Jon's face contorted to a less inviting look. "There's nothing going on with me and her," he answered. "That kind of ended, maybe a few weeks after the little run-in I had with you and your brother. Add the thing with the Broken Skull, and it never got off the ground."

"The Broken Skull?" Emma asked.

"Don't you watch TV?"

"Not really."

Jon pursed his lips for a second and then said, "This guy wears a mask and does unspeakable things to people. One night, he almost killed her."

"Does she have a name?"

"Yes. Daphne De La Rosa."

Emma smiled. The memories came flooding back. She remembered how pleased Jasper was when he returned from his encounter with the detective.

"What are you smiling about?" Jon asked.

"Nothing, just … you're single."

Jon asked, "What's so funny about that? Are you single?"

Emma frowned and rolled her eyes. "Perpetually."

Jon thought Emma was gorgeous, but successfully pushed away the urge to ask why she was single. Even though she and her brother seemed like bad news, she couldn't be involved in that *all* the time, could she?

Instead of prying, Jon shrugged and said, "Well, I guess we're two peas in a pod."

The table was quiet. They never ordered anything. The wait staff seemed to be unconcerned with breaking up the conversation. Jon was too focused on her snake-like charm. Emma was apprehensive about being completely open and honest with him.

Jon raised his hand. A waiter came by and took their order. He figured that would buy them enough time to think of ways to keep the conversation alive. They needed to change the subject, Jon thought.

"So, do you think the Broken Skull is like this big, powerful force out there?" Emma asked.

"He's definitely someone that needs to be checked," Jon said. "I used to collect everything I could on him when I worked at the department, like I would do something if ever confronted. If I didn't do anything to you or Patrick, I imagine I wouldn't be able to do anything to him. Maybe he'd trip over my dead body and sprain his ankle. That'd be my contribution."

"Maybe you just don't have the right motivation," she said. "You may surprise yourself, if there's something on the line you care about."

"Speaking of that, what motivated you to do what you do … used to do?" he wondered.

"Money, sometimes," she said. "Sometimes, the thrill. A lot of the time, Patty and I struggled. We got in trouble at school a lot, eventually got kicked out. Not long after that, our parents booted us. 'Good for nothing' was a popular word around the Starks household," she chuckled.

Jon nodded and took a sip of his drink. "That had to be pretty hard to hear."

"Yeah, but after a while, you get used to it," she said. "Someone tells you something enough, you start to believe it. Patrick never did, though. He'd always say we were fine, even when we weren't."

With a puzzled look on his face, Jon asked, "So, Patrick doesn't just punch people? He does other stuff?"

Emma laughed. "Yes." She touched Jon's hand. This time, he didn't move his hand. "He likes to read. He's very knowledgeable, if you ever end up having a conversation with him."

"Right now, he's the last person I want to have a conversation with," Jon said, "but I guess that implies I'll be around more than just this morning."

"I said it before: That's up to you," Emma said.

In unison, they asked, "So, how do I get a hold of you?"

Jon looked away, instinctively scratching the back of his neck to clear nervousness. He looked up shyly and said, "I have a number. I guess we could just …"

"Yeah. Let's just exchange numbers," Emma agreed. She gave him her number. He punched it in his phone and called her. She nodded when his number came up, and then he hung up.

"Easy."

"Do you have anything to do?" she asked Jon.

"Not really. Why?" he asked.

"Maybe we can just keep talking, if that's all right," she told him. "If we're talking, that means I'm not out getting into trouble."

Jon wasn't prepared for any of what was happening, or the speed in which it was happening. He admittedly was caught in the whirlwind. He found it hard to say no, even though that small twinge in the depths of his gut was telling him to.

Maybe he just needed to talk.

10

On another side of town, Markus was getting ready.

"Another self-destructive mission? So soon?" he heard over his shoulder. He turned around. Marissa sat up in the bed, the comforter pulled up to her chest. "Last night was a successful night. Why don't you come back to bed?"

"Look, it's obvious you're not happy with my lifestyle," he said to her. "Do you even want to know what happened, or are you just going to be busy being bitter?"

"The more I know the worse it is, but go ahead ... shoot," she said.

"She was attacked last night. That's why I was late."

Marissa's facial features softened at Markus's words. She didn't know much about Vanessa, but Markus cared about her, so she would understand the best she could.

Armed with that knowledge, she said, "Okay-okay ... well, what happened?"

"I'm not sure what happened. I haven't had much time to process it. From the looks of it, she was knocked off her bike and taken," he said.

"Do you know by who?" she asked.

"The Broken Skull."

The name sent shivers up her spine. Her dad said there was nothing to worry about, when she asked him about it. With someone like that, there was always something to worry about.

"How'd she get out?"

"I don't have that information," Markus told her. "What I saw was where she was. She was running down a road. The place was secluded. A van chased her. I got to her just in time. That van smashed into my car. She looked terrible when I got her."

Marissa nodded.

"I've never been responsible for anyone like this. I'm flying blind," he continued. "I don't know what I'm supposed to do, but what I do know is that I have to take care of her."

"Where is she now?" she asked.

"Downstairs, recuperating," he answered. "I looked over a couple times while she was in the passenger seat last night, and she had glass lodged in her face. She either jumped through a window, or got thrown. It's not clear."

Marissa whispered a curse word under her breath. "Are you going to go pick a fight? Be honest with me."

"I feel like he picked it first."

Markus walked out the door.

After 10 minutes, Marissa concluded she was done sleeping. She found herself at the basement door, contemplating whether she should enter. She leaned against the door and traced around the hand outline.

I'm just gonna do it.

She placed her hand on the sensor, granting her entry within seconds. After her short platform ride, Marissa guessed what room Vanessa was in. It was easy; all the other rooms were quiet and empty, except one.

The only light on faintly illuminated from Vanessa's chamber. She didn't know the content of Markus's chamber, but he seemed like new when he slept in it. She wondered if it worked for jet lag.

"I don't even know why I came down here," Marissa muttered to herself. She settled a few feet from the chamber. "I don't think you can hear me, but I want to let you know that … I'm not going to pretend to know what you've been through. I don't want to get in between what you two have, per se. Just understand that, as long as we're together, I'm going to be in the middle."

The chamber clicked open and slowly rose. Mist surrounded Vanessa's body, disappearing when she sat up. With her hand, she shooed some stray glass off her body, the shards falling into the chamber. She yawned and stretched.

She pointed at the chamber with her thumb. "I can hear through that thing."

She turned her body and rested her feet on the few steps that led down to equal ground with Marissa. Up until now, it had never occurred to her how much bigger than Marissa she was. She guessed she was a few inches taller, about 30 pounds heavier.

Marissa smiled politely. "Well, is there anything you want to discuss about it?"

"Not really," Vanessa replied. "You were clear. You have the way you feel, and I have mine. Believe me, we're on the same page."

"What do you mean?"

"Well, you said you were going to be in the middle. I think you're wrong. Actually, I know you are."

Marissa half-grimaced, half-narrowed her eyes. She then asked, "How am I wrong?"

Vanessa descended down the steps of the chamber and passed Marissa. She looked in the mirror, eyed down Marissa through the mirror's reflection. "Well, with all due respect, he found me. He also trained me. He wants me around. I'd advise you to be prepared for *me* to be in the middle, as long as he's The Sound."

"You have a good point," Marissa said. "But he can't do this thing at night forever. Nobody can."

"He may not be able to do it forever, but you're not so naïve to think we haven't bonded?" Vanessa questioned.

"I believe you two have bonded … but not like us," Marissa shot back. "We didn't meet in a life-or-death situation. We met under a normal one."

Vanessa chuckled and said, "As if I had control over how we met."

She dipped her head and washed her face. She'd been sleeping for hours. She felt the "tired" all over her face. She also felt the rising anger on her face. She turned around and faced Marissa.

"I wonder how you'd feel if you were forcibly knocked off a bike, drugged with something that I still don't know what, and then held down to be asked who The Sound is."

"Yeah, b–"

"No. I'm not finished," Vanessa interrupted. "I wonder if you could fight your way out of captivity, not against one, but against three, all while avoiding getting knifed. I wonder if you'd have the mettle to jump through a window when you don't see another way out, and sprint your way to safety."

She walked past her.

"Hopefully, your party went well. I'm sorry if Markus was late; he was busy making sure I wasn't murdered," she called behind her, grabbing the doorknob. She slammed the door and walked toward the escalator. Out of the shadows came Markus. She tried to pass him, but he stepped in front of her.

"What just happened?" he asked, concerned.

Vanessa looked at Markus and sighed. "Nothing. Well, something. I'm quite done with your girlfriend assuming the worst every time our names are brought up in the same sentence," she told him. "It's not some kind of love triangle. It's not. I want my respect, Markus. If she's too immature to understand that you and I have to have some kind of relationship to do what we do, then that's just too bad. I'd die for you, Markus. I think you would, me. Would she do the same for you?"

He looked past her. She turned around. Marissa was standing there.

"Impeccable timing, as usual," Vanessa said, sliding past him and up the platform.

Markus stood alone with Marissa. She apprehensively approached. Her voice was soft when she said, "So … Vanessa told me what happened."

"Did she?" Markus asked.

"Yeah. Listen, can you tell me what that thing does?" she asked, pointing at the Recovery Chamber.

"It recognizes all the bad things in your body and takes them out. She was injected with something, and it was forcibly pulled from her pores, like a detox. There was some glass lodged in her skin, too. That also got pulled out. After that, it speeds up the healing process. Trust me, she looked a lot worse last night."

"It does all that?"

"Yeah. I'd have scars, if not for it."

"Okay. Hey Markus, can I ask you something?"

"Sure."

"Is there enough room for both of us in your life? I mean, Vanessa and me? Don't hold it against me for asking this, but … if you had to choose, who would you choose?"

He shook his head. "That's not fair. I– … that's not fair."

"It's a simple question, Markus."

"I know it's a simple question. The answer isn't."

"Then simplify it for me."

"Okay."

Marissa nodded at Markus's agreement and smiled.

"We need to break up."

11

They looked at each other through the silence. She wondered what was going on in his head. His words seemed so off-the-cuff. She figured if she stared at him long enough, he would eventually speak again. He didn't.

"Okay, so that's it?" she asked, finally putting an end to the standoff.

"Yeah."

"I need you to explain this to me. You're not getting off that easy. Explain."

"There's really nothing to explain," Markus said.

"So you're picking her."

"My first priority is keeping the streets safe. That includes you. It was that way before we got together."

"What?" she said arrogantly. "You think I'm going to get hurt, or something?"

"No. I think you'll get killed."

Marissa cocked her head forward and blinked a couple times. "Excuse me?! Killed?!"

"Yes. I can't afford for anyone to know my identity. If that happens, people I love will be in danger. I trusted you enough to tell you my biggest secret. I'm still trusting you to hold on to it."

Marissa raised her eyebrows and said, "Oh, you're still serious about this."

"Yeah. I've been thinking about it since we got together."

"Then why are you leading me on?!" Marissa spat. "Did you think I'd be satisfied calling you my boyfriend for a few months? So basically, I just wasted months of my life worrying about you. Is that it?"

"You were worrying about me before then," Markus said.

"That's not the point!" she shouted. "That's *so* not the point!"

"Look, do you want to stay here, or should I make arrangements, or … what do you want me to do?" Markus asked.

"It's not right to stay here anymore. I don't feel welcome," she said.

Markus shook his head. "You are always welcome here, Mare. You know that."

"No, I don't. I'll send for my things in the morning, if that's okay with you."

"Okay. Not a problem," he said.

"It's crazy how one suit can make you a completely different person," she said. She just missed his shoulder as she passed him, headed to the platform.

"I've always been this way. Maybe it just slipped your mind."

She turned toward him again. "I loved you, even before you unnecessarily started risking your life. Maybe that slipped *your* mind."

She turned around again. After the platform worked toward the main level, he heard the basement door shut.

"I made the right decision," Markus told himself. Whether it was the smart decision or not, he would leave that to someone else to decipher. For now, he would live with it, and possibly, the realization of living his life alone.

Around late morning, Vanessa pushed her home's door open. There sat Jasper, who'd recently earned a key to her place. As soon as he saw her, he popped off the couch and embraced her tight. She embraced him back. He spoke in a low tone.

"I didn't hear from you all night."

They broke their embrace. "Everything is fine," Vanessa said, "but you look a little worse for wear." She observed a small bruise on his cheek. She moved to caress his face. "What happened?"

Jasper laughed and moved his face away. "A patient hit me. In-house visit. I didn't see it coming. That hasn't happened in months. I usually stay right outside arm's reach with patients, but … I guess it just slipped my mind."

"Well, at least get some ice, will you?" Vanessa asked. "How long have you been settled here?"

"Maybe an hour," he replied. "I was worried about you. The streets aren't very safe these days."

"Yes, I know. I try to stay off them, when I can."

"So, where were you?" he grilled.

"Working late," Vanessa said quickly. "I have a couch in my office. I just slept there. Just stopping through to freshen up and nap before work calls again."

"You should tell Mr. Doubleday you need a day off," Jasper insisted. "God knows you need one."

"Oh, no … no rest for the weary," Vanessa said.

She opened her refrigerator and poured herself and Jasper a glass of water. Even prepared a small ice pack for him. She tossed him the ice pack and placed his glass of water on the counter.

"Vanessa, I have something to tell you, and I don't want it to get weird, so bear with me," he told her. "Here, take a seat with me."

He sat, then her.

"I'm not who you think I am. I'm not even who I think I am."

Vanessa visibly tensed up. She had her hand on his knee, but slowly started to retract it. Jasper placed his hand on top of hers and gently tugged on it. He looked at her while he collected his thoughts.

Then, he said, "I love you."

That wasn't exactly what Vanessa was expecting. The hand she had on his knee squeezed his kneecap.

"I was really worried last night," he continued. "That's how I knew how I felt about you, when I sat up and waited and deliberated. I was definitely concerned."

"So, you just sat up like a bump on a log, thought about our relationship, and landed on 'I love you'?" she shook her head and shrugged. "That's something."

"Are you upset about something?" Jasper asked.

"No, not at all. Just seeing what your motives are. Both my parents are gone, and the last thing I need is for someone else to leave. I don't know if you should commit so early."

"I can't help what I want, Vanessa. In hindsight, maybe I should've kept it to myself. I don't believe that would be fair to either of us, though. You may have hang-ups. We all do. I'm willing to support you. Hopefully, you'd do the same for me."

Their lips met and locked. When Vanessa pulled back, she said, "So you're not in the dark, I do love you. I'm not saying it just because you said it, so don't think that."

"Understood."

"Tonight seems like a movie night. What do you think? A night in, you and me …"

"That sounds good."

"Maybe you can graduate to my bed tonight? You probably don't want to sleep on my couch again, do you?" she smirked.

"No. Actually, I'm glad you said something. I was going to start bringing an inflatable mattress."

She chuckled. "In all seriousness, thank you for being so patient with me," Vanessa said. She kissed him again. "I'm glad you approached me at the restaurant that day."

"I'm glad I went to the Crooked Tree today."

Jon was putting the finishing touches on his hair. The longer hair was a little more maintenance, but ultimately, he'd made the decision to keep it. It suited him better than his short hair, he thought.

He was waiting for Emma to arrive. He was excited about the possibility of a connection, even though he still had some hang-ups about how they met in the first place.

A knock at the door brought him out of his thoughts. He looked at his reflection. "Yes." Jon jogged over to the front door and opened it. "Hey …" he dropped his eyebrows. "Daphne? What are you doing here?"

They both looked at each other.

"You smell good."

"Thank you," he said shortly. "I'm expecting company. I can't really talk right now."

"Well, do you mind holding off on it for about an hour, maybe? I need your help."

"With what?" Jon asked.

"I need help getting The Sound's attention."

Jon unknowingly slid his shoulders back and cocked his head up. "I don't know how to get his attention, Daphne. Plus, after what you said about what you'd do when you caught him … I just don't see the incentive."

"I'm not going to do anything," Daphne said.

"You didn't say that before," Jon said.

"I know what I said," Daphne replied, her voice raised. She stopped herself, closed her eyes and exhaled. "I just wanna talk to him, one-on-one. You read enough comic books to know what's going to get him to show up."

"Daphne, seriously? Those are comic books," Jon shot back.

"Jonathan, please … we need his help."

Jon stopped being argumentative when he heard his name spoken like that. She always called him by his last name or nothing at all. It had to be serious.

"Okay, I guess I'll do what I can."

Daphne nodded her head. "Yes. I knew I came to the right person. Thank you."

Jon only nodded. He slid his shoes on and grabbed his keys. "We can drive separately. Like I said, I'm expecting company, and I don't anticipate this taking long."

"No, it's okay," Daphne said.

He followed her down the hallway and onto the elevator. They didn't say anything, electing to stand in silence on the ride down. When they landed on the main floor, they both got in their cars, and Jon followed her.

He took a moment to shoot a text to Emma.

Hey. Something came up. Sorry about that. I'll be home later. Shouldn't take long.

After he sent that text, a quick one came back.

Okay, no worries.

He smiled at her text. His guardedness was slowly slipping away.

Before he knew it, Jon found himself parked on the side of the road. De La Rosa's car was parked in front of his. Jon followed Daphne into an alleyway. After several feet, they stopped. An uneasiness set in over him, but he tried his best to hide it.

"Okay, so why are we here?" Jon asked. "What do you need me to do?"

"I was wondering … can you just act really scared?" Daphne asked.

"What? What's that even mean? How do you want m–"

Daphne ripped her gun from the back of her pants and pointed it at him. Her gaze changed from inquisitive to intimidating.

"Whoawhoawhoa! Hold on! What's going on?!" Jon placed his hands up. His eyes wide as half-dollars, he said, "Daphne, wait … just wait. I think there's been a misunderstanding."

"No there hasn't."

She held her gun steady, ripping four quick and consecutive shots from her gun. Jon fell to the ground immediately. Daphne took a few steps toward his body and unloaded three more shots. She held the gun to her side and looked at Jon's face.

She heard a sound. She swung around.

"I knew you'd show."

She looked him up and down.

"When did you decide you didn't like him anymore?" The Sound asked.

"I've always liked him," she said. "I may not agree with everything he says, but I've always liked him."

Jon moved. The Sound noticed. He also noticed no blood on Jon's clothes. He looked around the scene.

"No way out this time," she said, pointing her gun at him. "Don't even think about it."

It finally dawned on Jon that Daphne used him to get close to The Sound. He shook his head and looked at his hero.

"I-I'm sorry," he said. "She said she just wanted to talk to you. If I thought she would do something like this, I would've never agreed to it. I–..."

"Shut up!" Daphne snapped. She turned her attention back to The Sound, pointed her gun and pulled the trigger.

Nothing happened. The top of her gun was ripped off, clean. Daphne's poise was nonexistent as she turned the gun, gripped the barrel, and swung as hard as she could at him.

He dodged it.

With her other hand, she grazed his chin with a punch and swung her gun again. He popped her in the wrist with his palm. The sharp pain made her drop her gun. He kicked it away. She threw another punch at him. He grabbed her wrist and flipped her over his body. Her body slapped the ground. She looked up at him, enraged.

"Move in! Move in!" she yelled at the top of her lungs.

Lots of eyes and pointed guns. He looked up at the rooftop. More eyes, more guns. Lots of words thrown around. All of it was a blur. He closed his eyes for a moment, and then opened them. He looked down at Jon.

"I'm sorry. I'm so sorry," the young man said.

Taking a deep breath, The Sound raised his hands. Daphne grabbed his wrists and roughly put them behind his back.

She spoke through her teeth when she told him, "Add assaulting an officer to your list of offenses." She slammed him against a nearby wall, pressuring his body with her weight. "You're going to pay dearly."

Two officers grabbed him by the arms and escorted him to a police cruiser. While he walked, he looked toward the rooftop. Guns were still pointed his way. The barrels followed him all the way to the backseat of the cruiser. The windows were tinted. It looked like 0%. He thought it was very unusual. Nonetheless, he followed orders.

Back in the alleyway, Jon stood with Daphne.

"You did the right thing," Daphne assured him. She moved her hand toward him to console him. He took a step away from her.

"No I didn't. You lied. I thought I could trust you. What happened to you?"

Daphne said, "Nothing. Just finally woke up, that's all. You – of all people – shouldn't be surprised. You knew what I stood for. Did you think that would change, all of a sudden?"

"Yes."

"Well, you thought wrong."

"You can't tell me you're not the least bit worried about that guy," Jon said. "He's a human being. And despite all that, you're willing to hurt – or even kill – someone who is doing a justice to this world. I don't believe that. You may have changed, Daphne, but I don't believe you've changed so much that the badge is used to just … push an agenda."

"I'm sorry, are you trying to change my mind about something I said I was going to do and actually did?" Daphne questioned. "Deadmarsh, you're not a detective anymore. *Your* choice, not mine. You know what that means?" she asked. Before he answered, she said, "You're just another guy on the street, as far as I'm concerned. If I have to lie to you to get what I want, I'll do it."

Jon shook his head no at her words.

"I thought I was more than just another guy to you, no matter what job I had," he said. "Maybe that's why I don't fight on your side anymore."

"Admit it: You don't fight on my side because you're too soft for it," Daphne said. "You were starstruck when he showed up. If it were up to you, you'd let him go without so much as a peep, so spare me, okay? Spare me." She briskly walked away, shaking her head.

Jon watched the alley clear out. He eyed so many officers on their way out, he lost count. He wanted to get across that he was disappointed in them, but they didn't seem to notice or care.

When the coast was clear, the alleyway was quiet again. Jon glumly took in his surroundings.

"I have to get out of here," he muttered to himself.

During his walk, Jon replayed the night's events in his mind over and over. He should've stood his ground, stayed back. What would De La Rosa have done? Would she take drastic measures earlier? Would she bring him to the alleyway by gunpoint? Would the scene have gone any other way than the way it went?

He tried every possibility on the quiet ride home, with an added thought: She clearly tricked him when she apologized for her behavior in the past. She looked and sounded so sincere, but it was all for nothing.

By the time he broke out of his over-analytical funk, his eyes were on Emma Starks in the hallway, waiting at his door. He scratched his head.

"Hey, ummm … what are you doing here?"

"I wanted to surprise you. I didn't have anything else to do, but then you weren't home, and you weren't answering your phone." He nodded. She looked at him closer. "Is there something wrong?"

"Come in real quick," he ordered.

He unlocked the door and walked through. She followed. He turned around and looked past her. He strode past her, locked the door, and returned to his original landing spot.

"They took The Sound."

"I'm sorry … The Sound?" Emma asked, raising an eyebrow. "The guy? The crimefighter?"

"Yes. The police arrested him. I got used."

"You got used?" Emma asked. "By who?"

"Daphne … well, detective De La Rosa. The one you and your brother asked about when you came and knocked me out at the motel?" he asked.

"I know what my brother and I did before, but this that you're talking about … this is not my fight, Jon. I don't want you to dump your anger out on me because someone you love used you."

They stood in silence. He looked down, but he felt her eyes on him. He clenched his jaw and rubbed it, his hand over his mouth. He shook his head no.

"I have to do something."

"Why?" Emma asked.

"Because it's not right, Emma!" Jon barked. "It's not right. Let's face it, there aren't that many people that do good things in the world. This guy does … so I'm going to help him. I don't know how yet, but I'm going to."

"I know we're still getting to know each other, but I'm going to take a step back from this. Please don't hold it against me," Emma told him. "I want you to be able to trust me, so I owe you the truth: I'm not comfortable with this."

"Okay, uh … okay," was all he could muster. "Well, I guess I can meet back up with you when this is all over, or something."

"Before I leave … this has been going okay, right?" Emma asked, pointing back and forth between them.

"Yeah! Sure! Everything's fine," he replied. "I mean, it's only been a day, but … everything's fine, Emma. I'll see you soon."

"Okay."

She hesitated at first, but decided to throw caution to the wind. She leaned in to kiss him.

He leaned back and held his hand out.

"I'm just not sure about that yet," he said. "It's a little fast for that."

Hiding the piercing disappointment the best she could, Emma used the short notice to throw a smile on her face as she shook his hand. The two looked at each other awkwardly - like both wanted to say something, but didn't - before she pulled away from the handshake and left.

When she shut the door behind her, she pulled out her phone and sent out a text.

DLR has the Sound. Deadmarsh boy told me. He's @ police station.

She pocketed her phone and smiled to herself as she walked down the hallway.

12

Sitting on his wrists, a masked Markus sat in the backseat. He worked and turned his wrists to try to gain comfort, but couldn't find any. He wasn't overly tall, but the backseat of the cruiser didn't seem built to handle anyone over six feet. The sound of chatter got Markus's attention.

"I can't believe The Sound is in our car," the officer in the passenger seat told the driver. He turned and looked in the backseat at Markus. "Unbelievable! I can't believe we finally caught you. We've been trying to catch you for years, and here you are." He turned back to the driver. "Hey, what do you think De La Rosa's going to do to him?"

The driver said, "I don't know. She's on a whole other level right now. No telling." He cocked his head up, looking in the mirror so he could see the backseat. "Hey tough guy, are you scared?"

The Sound remained silent.

"He's scared," the officer told the other. "I'm sure he's heard of what we do to guys like him that get caught."

Markus stared at the car's ceiling, watching the nightlights pass by as the wheels in his head spun. He had no backup, no ideas, and no way out. He spaced out for the rest of the car ride, hearing the chatter between the two officers, but not the words. Maybe he really *was* slipping.

Markus sat alone in a room, his wrists shackled to the back of the chair he sat in. They never unshackled him, they just added another set of handcuffs to lock him to the chair. From the way the officers treated him in the alleyway, he figured they weren't taking any chances with him.

De La Rosa strolled into the room.

"Before you get high and mighty, no, you don't get a phone call, and we're not booking you. All of this is off-the-record, like it never happened. So, you're going to answer our questions, no ifs, no ands, no buts. Is that understood?"

Markus didn't answer.

Daphne raised her voice when she said, "Is that understood?!"

He still didn't answer. Instead, he looked around the room.

"I'm going to assume you agree."

"One question, detective," Markus said.

"It'll be your only one, so make it good," she responded.

"Why haven't you unmasked me?" he asked.

"You want the truth?"

"Yeah."

She thought about it, then said, "I guess because … I don't want to humanize you. I know someone's under that mask, but if that mask stays on … I can convince myself you're the biggest POS out there. Then, I can do what I want to you without that pesky conscience."

He dipped his head and said, "What are your questions, then."

"Did you think you'd ever be caught?"

"No."

"Are you afraid of what we're going to do to the Ivory Fox when we catch her?"

"*If,* detective."

"We caught you, didn't we?"

"That doesn't mean you'll catch her. I showed you on numerous occasions, I'm not a threat to you or your precinct. I went quietly. If I wanted to put up a fight …"

"We would've filled your body full of lead."

"Or I would've dismantled every gunman you had, including you."

"Oh, really?" De La Rosa said, nodding her head. She slammed her hands on the table and pushed up to her feet. She rushed around the table and snatched up his jaw with her hand, forcing his head up with her vise-like grip.

"Is that what you think?!" she asked.

He closed his eyes.

"You think it's just that easy, huh? You're just going to … just dismantle us?!" she mocked. "Well, I got news for you."

She unholstered her gun and placed it to Markus's head. With her thumb, she cocked the hammer back.

"There's not a *damn* thing anyone would do about it if I pulled this trigger. I told you, I don't know who you are under that mask, and I don't care. I'm the wrong person to be a badass with. Cocky will get you shot, with me."

He opened his eyes and looked at her.

"Just do it. Stop threatening me and do it."

There was a knock at the door.

"One more second and I would've splattered your brains all over these walls."

She decocked her gun and holstered it. She backed her way to the door, keeping her eyes on him the whole time. When her arm bumped the interrogation door, she stepped out.

Someone else walked in and sat across from him.

"As per patient agreement, please make sure all microphones are turned off, and all officers wait outside until I knock."

"Turning off now," was heard over the room's loudspeaker.

He turned back, looked across the table. "Looks like you're in big trouble," he said. "I want to help you out of this. Maybe we can find a way to compromise. First things first: My name is Jasper Kane."

13

"I know who you are," a masked Markus said. "You've been on TV and the radio before."

"Do you know why I'm here?" Jasper asked him.

"No."

"Because … I want to help you find what you're looking for. I have a technique called Soul Searching. You need to feel safe to open up. Call it a natural cleanse. It won't take long, trust me."

Jasper slowly stood up from his chair and rounded the table. Markus tensed up.

"It's okay," Jasper assured, sending a message of submission by raising his hands up a few inches. He placed his hands on The Sound, pressuring his cheeks with his thumbs. "Let me look into those eyes of yours."

He gazed into Markus's eyes, then said, "Can I share something with you?"

Silence.

"I'll take that as a yes. You're in a compromising position, anyway." His voice changed when he whispered, "I almost killed your partner."

Markus's heart started to race. He looked into Jasper's eyes. The pieces were coming together. He remembered the times he'd zoom in, look at the Broken Skull's eyes. The same color, the same intensity … he wanted to shake loose and go after him. They could end it now; they could end it tonight. Instead, he was stuck.

"I see I've got your attention. I told you we'd meet soon, friend." Jasper's thumbs dug into his subject's cheeks. "So, while you're here … I'm going to go out there, I'm going to find her, and I'm going to kill her." He nodded his head yes with his words and grinned.

"I'll get out of here," Markus growled, "and when I do, I'm coming for you."

"You'll be here as long as the police want you here," Jasper said, pulling his thumbs away from his adversary's face. "There's no bail for you, and they're not telling any news outlets. This situation is a lot worse for you than it sounds."

The Sound's tone was low when he asked, "How so?"

"Chances are, depending on where they put you … you could get beat to death in here," Jasper told him. "Some of the things De La Rosa said about what she wants to do to you … it's not for the faint of heart."

"Didn't you try to kill her?"

"Kill her? I just tried to scare her," Jasper said. "If I really wanted to kill her, I would've. I could've killed her and Detective Deadmarsh, but didn't. And why do you think that is?"

"You want to stretch this out."

"Precisely. I do what I want, when I want, and now … you're no longer standing in my way."

"Why don't you just take my mask off? Then you'll know who you're dealing with."

Jasper crept closer.

"Because it's much more fun to figure out the puzzle that is The Sound." Once he was done, he backed off and gave Markus a knowing nod. "Thank you for this," Jasper said, placing his hands together in a prayer pose, dipping his head. He then turned and walked toward the door.

"Wait ..."

Jasper turned around. "How else may I assist you?"

"She's tougher than me," The Sound told him.

"Is that a fact?" Jasper asked.

"Yeah. If you seek her out, she'll destroy everything you've built."

"How so?"

"She's angrier, got less to lose ... I could go on all night, but it's better you see for yourself."

Jasper stalked back to the vigilante, standing over him. "We apparently think differently. I don't care what she's got to lose. She's going to die, and there's nothing you can do about it."

Jasper left. The Sound sat motionless in the chair. The gears of his mind were hard at work as he formulated escape plans. He needed to get out, but how?

The door opened again, just as soon as it closed. De La Rosa walked in, flanked by two officers. They were bigger than he was used to seeing. He eyed them, but their eyes were already on him.

"They're going to take you to your cell," De La Rosa mentioned. "Do me a favor: Resist."

More silence. The two men unshackled him from the chair, then forcefully pulled him to his feet. Their grip tightened with every step. Markus sensed they'd already come in half-cocked. They didn't need a reason to rough him up, and weren't looking for one. He was at their mercy.

They shoved him into the holding cell and slid the cell closed.

"What'd you say?" one of the cops said. The officer opened up the cell again, scoffed to himself. "No, what did you say?!" he asked him again.

The Sound showed his hands to the officer, as an act of nonviolence. The officer unsheathed his baton and swatted the vigilante in the side of the leg, dropping him to a knee. The next swat found his face. The hero instantly tightened up into a ball, using his arms and hands to cover his head.

Then he felt a second baton. And a third. They worked in unison, but every strike was nuanced. Different-sized men, different-sized damage. Markus's body felt the intentional harm behind their swings.

Markus didn't open his eyes until he heard the cell door shut. Still covered up, he looked around as much as he could. Even though his suit protected him from most things, repeated blows wasn't one of them. He made a mental note to check on increasing the durability of his suit while he scanned his surroundings. The only pair of shoes that remained belonged to the man sitting in the cell with him.

"They're gone, man. You all right?"

Markus slowly stretched his limbs out and looked at the ceiling. "I'm okay." He took a deep breath in and exhaled out. While he assessed the damage by pushing on different parts of his body, he said, "I know you from somewhere. We've met before."

"I know you the Sound dude," he said. "I'm Leonard Robinson, and I'm a damn good information salesman. We've traded goods and services before. I'm afraid I don't have any in stock, whatever fancy thing is on your wrist."

Markus brought his wrist up. All the buttons were busted. He got to keep his life, but in return, his main option for escape was taken off the table. He looked at the ceiling again.

"So … you gonna get up?" Leonard asked.

"I don't know," he replied.

"You gotta know, man! You supposed to be The Sound, right? Crime fighter and everything?"

Markus nodded yes.

"Well, how come you ain't fight back?" Leonard asked. "You should've fought back. Everything I hear about you … I don't know why you didn't."

"I'm not the enemy they want me to be," he responded. "I could've taken drastic measures against them, but that would just get me killed. That's what they want. I just need to stay alive."

"I see your point. Hey, why you so open with your feelings and everything, though?"

"Because…" Markus paused and collected his thoughts, then said, "If they kill me in here, I want someone to know why I'm doing what I do."

"Aw man. Appreciate that!" Leonard beamed. "I feel honored."

"It's by default. You're the only one here," he responded.

Leonard immediately frowned. "And you didn't even have to say that."

Vanessa hadn't heard a thing from Markus all night. She paced and periodically checked her phone. She'd called him a few times. Oddly, she wasn't used to being the one to call him.

"It might just be a quiet night," she argued with herself. She sat on her couch, but popped up just as soon as her butt hit the cushion, starting to pace again. Deep down, her growing anxiety nagged her, feasted on her thoughts.

A knock at the door brought a welcoming distraction. She looked in the keyhole before opening the door.

"Hello there," Jasper said to her. Vanessa half-heartedly kissed him, managing an equally half-hearted smile.

"Something wrong?" he asked.

"Just got a lot of things on my mind," Vanessa said. "Do you mind to shut the door?"

"Sure."

After Jasper shut it, they plopped on the couch. She crossed her legs and rested the side of her head on his bearded jaw. He put his arm around her.

"Just an odd night," Vanessa said. "Something about tonight, I'm not sure what. It's just going to stay odd, I guess."

"Well, I don't know if there's anything I can do, or …"

"No, I'm not sure there's anything you can do. It's just … Markus usually calls about something work-related and hasn't, that's all."

Jasper raised his eyebrows an inch, and then dropped them. "I'm sorry, I'm not following. Does he call every night?"

"Yeah, usually. We reflect on how the day went and anything big on the schedule coming up. I'd say I'm his eyes and ears."

Jasper's shrug and sigh worked in harmony. "He may have just forgot. He's a busy guy, right? I don't think Markus became a billionaire by sitting around."

Vanessa sighed. "I guess you have a point."

"Relax with me tonight. I'm sure he's got enough money and resources to feel comfortable, wherever he is. Let me help ease your mind."

Vanessa peered at Jasper. "And how do you plan to do that, Mr. Kane?"

He turned his eyes down her way and beamed.

"Well, the night is fairly young. We have our youth, right?"

Vanessa laughed and said, "You're quite a ways older than me. I'm afraid youth isn't on your side anymore."

Jasper looked offended. "Just because I'm closer to 40 than you are to 30 …"

Vanessa placed a hand on his chest. "Oh, don't be like that. Besides, I accept your offer. Hopefully, that'll quell your ego."

Vanessa pat his chest exactly one time, then stood up. Jasper followed her steps. She felt excitement in her fingertips with every movement toward the bedroom. She wondered if Jasper felt the same.

As one door shut, another opened.

Jon stomped into the detective's office. The office didn't really stop, so much as glance up momentarily. He looked around the office for De La Rosa, but so far, there was no sign of her.

"Didn't you quit?" one said.

"I'm looking for De La Rosa. That's it," Jon said.

"She had to step away for a minute. I can leave a message," he offered.

"I can wait," Jon countered.

"I don't think you should. Actually, I don't know how you got back here, anyway. You're a civilian now. You need to go about your business."

"Are you in on it, too?" Jon asked.

Clearly annoyed, the detective stood up from his desk and approached. Jon never wavered. Now standing face to face, Jon felt the detective's breath hit his upper lip. While he breathed through his nose, he'd stopped blinking seconds ago.

"I know you don't wanna start nothing in here," the detective told him. "You got no friends around here." Looking at Jon quizzically, he said, "Wait … you think because you grew a little facial hair that you magically grew a set, too?"

Jon stayed calm. The detective nodded.

"You're the same as you always were, just a soft-ass punk. Do something."

"That's enough, detective," Jon heard behind him.

His stubborn eyes remained stuck to the disrespectful former detective in front of him. This was his moment to prove he wasn't going to take anything from anyone anymore. The detective in front of him was the pinnacle of all the things that made Jon hesitate. Not today.

"Deadmarsh … come with me," he heard.

He blinked. The detective in front of him acknowledged it with a knowing shake of the head. Feeling the tug on his arm, Jon relented, allowing himself to be pulled into De La Rosa's office.

"Please sit down," she said.

"I really don't want to, Daphne," Jon said.

"Okay, let's stand. Why are you here?"

"Did you let The Sound go?" he asked.

"Jesus! Will you keep it down?!"

In between her words, Daphne forced her way past Jon, violently slamming her office door. "Did I already let him go?" Daphne repeated, turning the wands to close her office blinds. "No. There's no reason to. I know what you said about it, but we're not going there. Now, unless you have some other business here, I suggest you leave."

Defiant, Jon crossed his arms. "I'm not leaving."

Much like one of the detectives did minutes ago, Daphne stood in front of Jon. "No, Deadmarsh … you're leaving. I promise you won't like what happens if you stay."

"Spare me, with your cryptic words," Jon said. "You seemed a lot bigger when you were in charge of me."

Jon's cutting words caught Daphne by surprise. The surprise in the way this interaction was going quickly made her angry.

"What's that mean? I'm small, now?" she asked.

"Well, yeah. That's the inverse."

Jon's words dug into Daphne's emotions. She found herself angrier with every retort. While she gathered her thoughts, they continued to be interrupted by deeper thoughts, about how somehow, they'd lost each other along the way. The exchange was too heated for a return to civility.

Finally, she blurted out, "Do you want me to arrest you?"

Jon's smirk faded. "You wouldn't do it."

"Oh, I wouldn't?" she said. "I'm the law around here. That didn't change when you quit. The beat goes on, Deadmarsh. If you came to beg me to release your little friend, it's not happening. Who are you going to call? The police? The madder you make me, the worse I'll make it for him. Catch my drift?"

"Spell it out for me."

Daphne abruptly rushed him, grabbing two fistfuls of his collar. She pressed him against the wall. She felt him attempt to pull away. She tightened her grip and pressed harder.

"I can throw your ass in that cell. Tread lightly."

Even though he felt her knuckles pressing into his neck, he still managed to move his eyes to hers. "If you need to throw me in a cell for speaking up , then do what you need to do."

"Fine."

She pulled out a pair of handcuffs with one hand, turned him around with the other.

"Jonathan Deadmarsh, you're under arrest for obstruction of justice."

She read him the rest of his rights as she tightened the shackles around his wrists. He mouthed every word. She opened her office door and nudged him through, keeping a hand on him as a guide.

They headed toward the basement, a place Jon wasn't familiar with. He never needed a reason to be. What was down there? Two doors later, Jon found himself being jabbed down a dark corridor. As he passed brick after brick, Jon noticed a drop in temperature. Nervousness washed over his body.

"Ummm …. so … when do I get my phone call?" Jon asked.

"If you make it down here, you don't get one. Keep walking."

She nudged him hard. Jon nodded his head in disapproval. As he neared, he saw Leonard Robinson and The Sound, sitting in a single cell. It was grimy, old and unclean. It smelled just how it looked. De La Rosa opened the cell door and sarcastically motioned for Jon to keep walking. He didn't resist, just walked in and leaned up against the wall.

"You sure this is the way you wanna go?" Jon asked.

Daphne slammed the cell door shut. "*You* chose to play it this way. Don't ask for something, and then get mad when you get it."

Daphne didn't waste any time walking away from the cell and back down the corridor.

"Man, I never thought I'd see *you* in here!" Jon heard. He turned his head and looked at Leonard. "Ain't you one of them? What they got you in here for?"

"Obstruction," Jon replied. "I accidently helped lure him into police custody," he said, listlessly pointing at The Sound.

Leonard's face scrunched up, perturbed. "Man, how you 'accidentally' do something like that?"

Jon looked up to see multiple officers shuffling down the hallway. As they closed in, their batons showed. Jon counted seven.

"What are you guys doing?" Jon questioned.

No answer came. Instead, a few of them squeezed into the cell.

"Hands against the wall," one of them commanded.

"But we didn't do anything," Jon argued.

"Hands against the wall!" the officer repeated, his voice raised.

"Tell us what we did!" Jon pleaded, his voice matching the officer's pitch.

The officer jammed his baton into Jon's ribs. He clutched his abdomen and quickly hit the ground. One more swipe from the baton found a piece of his arm, but most of his shoulder. The attacking officer stood over Jon and sneered.

"Okay! Stop!" Jon cried. He rolled to his back and brought his knees up. Another swat stung his leg. He yelled out in pain and rolled to his side, ducking his head and closing his eyes. Then, he felt someone jump on him. He tried kicking them off, but the grip tightened.

"Stop moving or they'll kill you," he heard in his ear.

Repeated swats from the batons filled the room. As precious seconds passed, he heard the officers' breathing get heavier and heavier. As suddenly as it started, it stopped. Jon listened to the steps retreating from the cell. A motionless Sound slid off Jon and lay on his back.

"That will do."

Jasper Kane. Jon recognized him from TV, even copied some of his psychiatric style. Jon wondered if Jasper was part of the new approach at the police department.

Jasper stepped over him and dropped into a squatting position beside The Sound. He whispered a few words into The Sound's ear, patted him on the chest and went to stand up, but stumbled. Jasper quickly steadied himself, using one hand to plant on The Sound while the other hand gripped the cell. The officers rushed to help, but Jasper refused it, pulling himself upright.

"Hopefully, he makes the right decision," Jasper told Jon and Leonard.

When Jasper left, Leonard surveyed the scene. He purposely looked at the former detective out of the corner of his eye, curling his lip, as well. Shaking his head, he knelt down beside The Sound.

"The way he did you, and you jumped on him to protect him?" he asked. "Man, that's crazy. Ain't no way in hell I'm taking an ass-whoopin' for someone that got me caught up. No way in hell."

The Sound didn't respond.

"I didn't mean to," Jon shot back. "De La Rosa tricked me. I shouldn't have even been there. She told me she just wanted to talk to him. I believed her. She never gave me a reason not to."

Jon looked at The Sound.

"Until last night."

It got quiet in the cell. Jon started to say something, then stopped.

I need to say this.

Throwing his hands at his sides, Jon said, "Whoever you are, I'm sorry. I broke Superhero Code by trusting someone that was looking for you. I shouldn't have done that. I'm so sorry."

"Things happen," The Sound said. "And Leonard ..." He rolled over. "I jumped on him because it was the right thing to do," he said. "It defeats the purpose, to sit back and let things happen around you."

"Even if it might kill you?" Leonard asked.

"Yeah."

The Sound slowly moved his hand over to Jon's and rapped his knuckles, as if knocking. When Jon opened his hand, The Sound dropped a key and curled back up.

"Is this the key to the door?" he whispered.

"Yeah. There are two doors straight ahead: One to go through, and the second will come before a door that leads upstairs. In around eight minutes, transportation will be waiting for you. When I tell you to go, unlock the door and run. Don't look back."

"Man, you a straight-up G for this," Leonard said. "What about you, though?"

"I'll be fine," he said.

"You sure? Because we can always keep Deadmarsh here. He got you in trouble in the first place. Matter of fact, if you want me to, I can just knock this dude out right now."

Jon looked at Leonard. "Don't do … I'd rather that not happen."

"Me either," The Sound said. "Listen closely: As soon as you get to a phone, call this number. Don't text it. It's an associate of mine. They'll know what to do. No small-talk. As soon as they pick up the phone, start talking."

"What do you want me to do?" Leonard asked. "Sounds like he got all the jobs."

"Stay off the streets," The Sound grumbled. "Lay low and wait. I'll find you."

"All right, then! That's what I'm talking about!" Leonard smiled. "I knew you'd come through. That's something I can do!"

"Time to go," The Sound told them.

Jon nodded and fit the key inside the lock, minimally turning it. He turned and looked at The Sound one last time. With a click and a pull, the cell door opened. He turned back and faced the corridor and froze.

Just trust him. You owe him, Jon thought.

With Leonard right behind him, Jon ran down the corridor. He pushed one door open, then the other, the one right before the stairs leading up. A cab sat in the alleyway, emanating exhaust. He and Leonard pushed into the backseat. Neither were incarcerated for long, but that short time was enough.

"Excuse me sir," Jon said to the cab driver. "Do you have a phone I can use?"

14

Vanessa's phone buzzed.

She sleepily peered over her shoulder at Jasper. His back heaved and his shoulders shrugged. She assumed he was sleeping hard. Not long after he arrived, he complained about how tired he was. Vanessa had just fallen asleep a few minutes before her phone went off.

She lifted her head off the pillow and carefully sat up. She didn't recognize the number. She snatched up her phone and snuck out. When the bedroom door was shut and all was quiet, she answered.

"Hello? ... Yes, I am … Yes, I will. Goodbye."

Vanessa looked at the phone number again, as if doing so would help. She didn't know the number, but she knew the voice: Jonathan Deadmarsh, Detective De La Rosa's partner. She was sure her natural English accent threw him off.

"Who would call this late at night?" Jasper prodded, his eyebrows drooping. His voice made Vanessa slightly jump. "Couldn't have been the wrong number, could it?"

"No."

"Well, who was it?" Jasper grilled. "Don't tell me it was Markus Doubleday. You can't tell me he doesn't have a sense of time."

"When you're his assistant, you're on call. Right now, he's a little … piss drunk. I hate to run, but I need to pick him up and get him back safely."

She snatched her keys off the kitchen counter and walked to the door.

"Can I go with you?" she heard behind her.

She stopped in her tracks and turned around. "Well … no. I'll just be a minute, really. No need to make this a field trip, Love. Plus, I don't think he'd too much like the idea of a stranger seeing him at such a vulnerable moment."

"But you know me," Jasper said. "My intentions are genuine. I won't get in the way, I promise."

"You can be quite persuasive, Mr. Kane." She walked over and kissed him. "But the answer's still no. Be back in a jiff."

She walked to the door again.

"Be careful out there," she heard over her shoulder.

"Oh, you know me," she called over hers.

As Vanessa neared the Doubleday residence, his whereabouts dominated her thoughts. Her thumbs rhythmically tapped the steering wheel to the music in her car. She thought it would be easier to start at the house. Markus would appreciate her thinking.

"Peace First."

The basement lit up. Vanessa walked toward the computers that rose from their hiding place.

"Computer, I need to know where The Sound is."

A large hologram rose and rotated simultaneously. When it stopped, a few dots appeared on the screen. The word "Locating" blinked on and off. Seconds later, a solid black and blue dot popped up. Vanessa couldn't immediately pinpoint the location; the structure was still piecing together. When it finally finished, a label popped up.

"Police station. Bollocks," she muttered. "What kind of mess has he gotten himself into? God. Computer, is there more information?"

Another label appeared near the holographic precinct: Main Level. Vanessa observed where the blue line was. It looked to be underground.

"So, how am I meant to get him?" Vanessa questioned. "This is all a big mess. They're not just going to let me get him because I asked them nicely."

Another hologram popped up. The angle provided a first-person point of view. Out loud, she said, "Open the outside door … down a corridor … open another door … jail's right there. Sounds easy enough. Right. Cheers."

Vanessa waved her arms through the holograms until they disappeared. She walked toward the holders that housed her Ivory Fox suits.

"Well, time to make some enemies."

Drip. Drip.

Markus sat alone in the cell. The drip came through a crack in the wall. He couldn't bring himself to sleep. Water was offered to him, but he declined. He was paranoid enough to believe the police would poison him. Some officers were understanding, some weren't. He made peace with their approach years ago.

One of the officers offered Markus a bag of chips. "You think you'll rot in here?" he asked.

He declined the chips with a simple wave. "No. I have every intention of getting out of here."

"How? Nobody knows you're here. You won't eat or drink. You think De La Rosa will suddenly have a change of heart?"

"Maybe it'll hit her on just the right day."

"I don't know what day that is," the officer explained. "Listen, I don't know you, but … you seem like a pretty decent guy."

"Thank you."

"I don't know if I agree with you risking your life."

"You should. You do it because you want to help change the world. I'm not that different from you."

"You're different because you dress up in a costume and fight crime."

"So do you."

The officer grinned, then chuckled and shook his head. "Mine's a uniform," he said.

"Uniform … costume … something people don't usually wear to do something people don't usually do."

"Look, I don't wanna argue about this."

"We're just having a conversation. It's an opportunity to talk to someone outside your circle. Maybe we can understand each other better."

"Maybe. So, let me ask you: Is this something you love, like I love being an officer?"

Markus nodded yes. "I love knowing someone can walk down the street and feel a little safer knowing there's someone out there protecting them."

"Yeah, that's one of the reasons I took the job. I wanted to do my part. The badge means something to this city."

Markus pointed at his face. "So does my mask."

"Is that why you don't take it off?"

"I prefer not to, but if I remember correctly, your superior officer put out a strict order not to take my mask off."

The officer shook his head. "I didn't understand that then, either."

"She said she doesn't want to humanize me."

The officer looked puzzled. "Humanize you?"

"As long as I don't have a face, I'm just a thing," Markus replied. "Makes it easier for her to do what she's doing. I know she wants me to stop, but I can't. I know it's right."

"For the city's sake, I hope you survive this."

The officer moved a few feet down the corridor, swiping up a folded newspaper on the way. He sat in a single chair that sat against the wall and began reading.

Footsteps. Lots of them.

Markus blinked a few times and cocked his chin up, turning his head toward the corridor. The officer rose. The group pushed past him. In a matter of seconds, De La Rosa and her team were mere feet away from the single cell.

"Where are they?!" Daphne spat.

"At this point, they could be anywhere," Markus said.

Daphne got closer, clutching the cell bars tight. "Since you don't know where they are, why don't you tell me how they got out?!" she pressed.

"They used a key," he said.

"Where'd they get the key?" she asked.

"Somebody gave it to me."

"I need names, Mr. Moral High Ground!" she exclaimed. She turned and looked at the officer tasked with watching Markus, and then looked back. "Did he give it to you?" She turned again and approached the officer, pointing. "Did you give it to him?!"

"No! I mean … they were already gone when I made it down here! I guess … I guess I just didn't notice. I'm really sor–"

His words were cut off by a deep exhale. He didn't have time to brace for De La Rosa's impact. He dropped to a knee and looked up at the brunette, keeping himself balanced with one hand and clutching his stomach with the other.

"Two of the three in this cell are gone," Daphne said to the officer. "You didn't tell anybody, and sat down here, as if it was okay that there were people *missing*. Are you working with them?!"

"No! I don't even know them!" he said. "It was an honest mistake! It'll never happen again!"

She clenched her jaw and said, "You're damn right it'll never happen again. Go upstairs. *Now.*"

Still clutching his stomach, the officer stood up and wobbled down the corridor, receiving a couple shoves from Daphne's men as he ambled along. When he disappeared, Daphne turned her attention back to the mask in the cell.

"So … those two escape, and you stay. What's your play, here?" she asked him.

"There's no play," he told her. "I don't know about the other, but the Deadmarsh kid was detained for no reason. That gave him every reason to want out. I'm still here because this is where you wanted me. You didn't want them. You couldn't care less about them. You want me."

"And I always get what I want," she said.

"Why don't you just let me go, then?" he asked.

She turned to her cronies and said, "Leave us alone for a second." They nodded and shuffled down the hallway and through the doors.

"How do I get what I want if I let you go?" she asked.

"If you let me go, I'll go after the Broken Skull. Odds are, we'll end up killing each other. Two birds, one stone. That's what you want, right? To get rid of people like us? If we do it this way, your hands stay clean."

"I need to think on this."

Markus watched Daphne as she quietly deliberated his proposal. She alternated between looking at him, looking at the wall and looking at the ceiling. She looked at him one more time.

"It's like making a deal with the devil," Daphne said.

"For who?" Markus quipped.

"Considering your circumstances, it's impressive you still have a sense of humor." She pointed above her and said, "I'm going to go think about this. Give me an hour."

Markus nodded. Daphne left. When it was quiet again, Markus looked at his wrist and pushed buttons. Nothing happened. His wrist controls had been busted before, but checking again gave him an unexplainable comfort. He rested his back against the wall and sighed.

"One hour," he said to himself.

15

Vanessa pulled up to the police station.

"Looks about right," she said to herself. She walked up to the side door and worked her magic, unlocking the door in a jiff. She mentally walked herself through the computer's directions. She walked down the stairs, through the hallway, and through two doors. Then, she saw him from afar.

With a wide smile, she jogged over to him and said, "Fancy seeing you here."

"You too. We need to get out of here. She'll be back down soon." He reached through the cell bars and unlocked the door. They started their walk through the corridor. Markus moved noticeably slower. Vanessa put her arm around his waist.

"Are you all right?" she asked him.

"Not really. Hopefully, you fired up the R-3."

"I'm afraid I didn't. Had I known, I would've. Who did this to you?"

"De La Rosa."

She looked at Markus. "You mean, the best cop ever did this to you?" she said facetiously.

He looked forward. She followed his gaze. There she was.

She looked at Markus again. "Oh … wait … so … did she do this to you, or are you announcing her presence?"

"I did it to him," De La Rosa answered. She looked at her help. "Guys, no guns. We don't want to cause a commotion upstairs."

"Oh, it's jumped to this. All right." She turned to Markus. "How much are you going to be able to help?"

He shook his head. "You're going to have to take the lead."

"Right." She turned and smiled at him again. "Should be fun."

She turned her attention to the approaching officers.

"I would love to talk you out of this, but I fear I'd be unsuccessful," she said, watching their movements. "You know, you don't have to listen to De La Rosa about this." She shrugged. "You could totally just let us go."

They continued their approach, unresponsive to Vanessa's words. The only way out was through them. The one in the front threw the first punch. It didn't connect. Vanessa's fist exploded into his chest. He knocked over one of his cohorts, leaving the third. Coming forward, he tripped over the other two.

"Get up!" De La Rosa screamed at them.

They fought their way to their feet, pushing and shoving each other. The first threw another wild punch. With both her hands, Vanessa redirected him to the wall. While he struggled, Vanessa threw two kidney shots, then kicked him in the back of the leg, his knee slamming into the concrete wall. The bone-on-concrete collision dropped him in a hurry.

Screaming filled the corridor. Vanessa's back was turned when the second officer buried his fist into her ribs. Before the pain registered, she felt herself in a chokehold. She elbowed him to get space, then pushed away from the wall with her feet, slamming him against the wall. She threw her head back twice, the back of her skull hitting his teeth.

Definitely stitches, she thought.

She hit him again in the ribs. This time, he let go. She grabbed him by his collar and ran him into the other fallen officer. Both of their heads smacked against the concrete, knocking them out.

She turned and faced De La Rosa. "Would've been a lot easier if you just let us go. So, are you going to let us go, or am I going to have to knock you out, too?" Vanessa asked dryly. "Because I don't like you, so I'd take immense pleasure in it."

De La Rosa stoically stared at Vanessa. "I'd love to see for myself, but I'm going to let the targets eliminate themselves. Makes my job easier."

As Vanessa and Markus passed, she and the detective stared each other down. Vanessa didn't know what she meant. She made a mental note to ask Markus about it later. When she pushed the first door open with her foot, she turned toward Markus again.

"Are you right?" she whispered. "Looks to me like you need a proper shower and rest. That cell probably wasn't very comfortable."

"I don't think it's built for comfort," Markus said. A small grunt escaped.

"My bike is here. Are you good with riding on back? Will you be able to hold on?"

"Yeah."

"Good, then."

She pushed the second door open.

"There's blood on your suit," Vanessa said.

"I know," Markus replied.

"Yours or theirs?"

"Vanessa ..." Markus trailed off, struggling to catch his breath.

"Okay, right."

Vanessa's bike was running when they made it out the door. She sat on it and grabbed the handlebars. Markus gingerly found his way onto the bike. She felt Markus's tight grasp on her abdomen, followed by the side of his head resting on the back of her shoulder as she took off into the night.

As she cruised the nearly-bare streets, she smiled at the thought of saving Markus. She didn't have much time to talk to him - he wasn't in much shape to - but she was thankful she was able to find him.

Her tire burst.

The handlebars shook. Vanessa clutched them tight, fighting them to keep the bike straight.

"Lay it down!" Markus yelled.

She reluctantly shifted her body to one side as hard as she could. So did he. When the bike hit the ground, she let go. The bike skidded hard and far, sparks flying every which way. She felt the concrete eating at her suit as she slid, threatening to rip the fabric off her leg.

Vanessa and Markus finally slid to a stop. So did the bike. She slowly helped Markus to his feet, patting debris off his suit. He draped his arm around her shoulder.

"Are you right enough to take a stroll?" she asked him.

"I should be okay," Markus said.

"Good … because we have company."

Markus followed Vanessa's eyes. "The Broken Skull."

The Broken Skull approached the two, unhurried as he ground his fists into his palms.

"It's smarter to split up," Markus mentioned, taking his arm off Vanessa's shoulder.

"Are you mad? You're hurt," Vanessa whispered. "You need my help. We need to stay together."

The Broken Skull closed in.

"Split up," Markus told her sternly. "Now."

Vanessa glared at him, pursed her lips and shook her head no. "This is a mistake." She took off down the street, disappearing in seconds.

Markus turned his attention back to the Broken Skull. He estimated the Skull to be 20 feet away.

He turned and ran.

Pain raced through his body, piercing every step that pounded the pavement. He heard the Broken Skull's increased pace behind him. Jogging, but not a sprint. Markus kept his pace up, anyway.

Happening upon a fire escape, Markus jumped and grabbed rung after rung, continuing his climb to the top. Once there, he rested his hands on a concrete wall. He listened for the Broken Skull. He had no idea which way his enemy went. While he had time, he caught his breath and formulated a plan.

He heard the doorknob turn, watched the door open. It was him. Time was up.

The Broken Skull approached, stopping a few feet shy. He bobbed his head knowingly and highlighted his counterpart with a point. "I told you we'd meet soon."

"Why would you do this?" Markus asked, disregarding the Skull's words. "You've terrorized this city. You've killed people. What's the point of all this?"

"There really isn't one," the Skull told him. "I just go about this life, doing what I please. I cause chaos because I want to, plain and simple. You know … I could've killed you in that cell."

"Why didn't you?" Markus asked.

"I'm not certain De La Rosa would care."

"You really think she's that far gone?"

"I know she is," the Broken Skull said. "Did you think you'd be able to … talk her off the ledge, so to speak?"

"Yes, I did."

The Broken Skull chuckled. "You're more ambitious than I thought. Then again, you wouldn't have got this far without it."

A storm of punches flew Markus's way. He did his best to evade. Some slipped through. They tussled, hands grabbing each other's fabrics. Suddenly, Markus felt himself slammed against a wall. Then again. Then a third time. His legs buckled. Then, a rib shot. The next rib shot loosened his grip on the Skull.

Markus felt himself being forced to the ground. He tried to resist. The Broken Skull was too strong. The Skull straddled his torso, one knee up.

"You're no longer strong enough to defeat me," the Broken Skull said. "You never were." His hands gripped Markus's throat, growing tighter the more the hero squirmed.

Markus's eyes strained as he tried to conserve his breath. He punched the Broken Skull to create space, but it barely registered. The grip around his neck grew tighter. He tried to turn his hips, but the Broken Skull had him trapped. His eyes slowly rolled inside his head. The grip on the Broken Skull's jacket loosened. His hands slid down the Skull's jacket and hit the ground.

The Broken Skull was knocked back with so much force, he flew a few feet in the air. He rolled and caught himself.

"Idiot … did you really think I would leave him alone?" the Ivory Fox said. "Defeats the purpose of having a partner, don't you think?"

The Broken Skull stood up and dusted himself off.

"I thought you would. Self-preservation usually kicks in when I'm involved," he said, walking toward her. "If I have two targets, one will run. Perhaps you're the exception."

"It's getting late," the Fox said. "I've no time for monologues."

"Understandable."

He reared back. The Fox hit him across the jaw. He recovered quickly, but a left-right combo screamed his way, connecting again. She kicked him in the front of the knee, dropping him down. He looked up. Another left-right combo rocked him. Fierce anger adorned the Fox's punches, as if she hoped the next punch thrown would kill him. She threw another punch.

He caught it.

He followed with a punch that landed between the bridge of her nose and just above her eyebrows, sending her reeling. The back of her head smacked the pavement. She rolled over to her stomach.

The Broken Skull approached, but was distracted by The Sound's attempt to grab his ankle. He kicked away violently and looked down. "You are no match for me," he said. "Neither is she."

He grabbed the Fox by her shoulder, bunching up the top of her suit with his fist. Her head limply fell. He raised his other fist for the final blow. Her eyes slowly opened. He looked at her. Panic set in.

He released his grip and scrambled away from her, stopping when his back slammed against the ledge. With one hand, she touched her face all over. All she felt was skin. She gasped.

Markus slowly crawled over to Vanessa. Without breaking eye contact, he spoke over his shoulder.

"Do you want to tell her … or should I?"

16

Vanessa's eyes were still refocusing when she looked back and forth between the other two. She rubbed the area where she was struck. The pain shot into her eyes as soon as she touched the spot. She looked at the Broken Skull.

"Tell me what?" Vanessa asked.

The Skull stood at the ledge. She looked up at Markus.

"Tell me what?" she repeated, this time, louder.

The two men didn't answer. The Skull walked past.

"You're safe … for now," the Broken Skull called over his shoulder. "Next time, I won't be so lenient with your acquittance."

When he left, he slammed the exit door open with such force, it rattled the hinges.

"It seems we have a lot to discuss," Vanessa said.

Several minutes later, and the two found themselves inside Markus's garage after a quite bike ride.

"Where to? Recovery?" she asked him.

"I'm more hungry than hurt," Markus said.

"You're pretty hurt, from the looks of it."

Markus didn't respond to Vanessa's observation. Shrugging minimally, Vanessa gripped his waist and traveled up the platform escalator to the main level. Once there, she helped him to the couch.

"Do you have a preference?" she asked him, heading to the kitchen. She opened up his refrigerator.

"Should be a cup with some green stuff in it," he called.

Vanessa pushed some things around his refrigerator before she found the container Markus was talking about. "God, what kind of swill is this?" she muttered to herself. When she brought the container to him, he gripped the top and bottom, shaking it. He looked at it again, nodded, and guzzled it within seconds.

"Thank you," Markus said, handing Vanessa the container.

"So, no Recovery Chamber, I presume?" she asked, tossing the container in the sink.

"Not yet," Markus answered. "I want to be strong enough to get down there under my own power. I'm just going to rest here, for the time being."

"What was in that container, anyway?" she asked him.

"Everything you need," he answered.

Vanessa laughed. "Cryptic. Anyhow, you're in pretty good spirits, for just having a near-death experience," Vanessa said. She plopped down on one of the chairs near the couch Markus was on.

"I have near-death experiences every night. Nothing new," he said. "I could say the same about you."

Vanessa laughed. "But seriously, Markus … are you going to be all right?"

He turned his head slightly toward her. "Vanessa, I'll be fine. This isn't the worst thing that's ever happened to me."

"Hate to be a bother, but can we just acknowledge the elephant in the room and get it over with?" she asked him. "The suspense is quite killing me, if you haven't noticed."

"Can this wait until tomorrow?"

"Afraid not. Something about not wanting to go to sleep with something hanging over me. You understand."

"Okay." Markus studied Vanessa's features.

Her tone was more serious and concerned when she said, "With all due respect, sir … please stop yanking me around and get on with it."

"Jasper Kane came to visit me when I was in jail. He tried to get in my head, but I didn't budge."

She laughed nervously. "The suspense! For God's sake, spit it out, Markus."

"He's the Broken Skull, Vanessa."

Her shoulders tightened. She blinked and said, "This has to be a mistake. How could you possibly know he's the Skull?"

With irk in his voice, he said, "Your tone is a little accusatory."

"I couldn't care less what I sound like right now!" Vanessa said. "That's a little off, wouldn't you say? You mean to tell me that my boyfriend … my *boyfriend* … is walking around, murdering people? That's what you're telling me right now?!"

"He told me, Vanessa."

She pursed her lips, stared into his eyes. "I don't believe you."

Markus cocked his head sideways. "What *do* you believe? That I made this up?"

"It might've been a case of mistaken identity, for all I know. Maybe he was feeding you a line, trying to throw you off the trail of someone else."

"Or maybe he's just cocky," Markus countered. "Maybe he knows he has someone like you in his back pocket. Or even De La Rosa, for that matter. She might be in on it too, I don't know. But what I do know is that I don't have a reason to lie. Maybe your mask isn't the only thing that's covering your face."

"Rude. That's very, very rude." Vanessa stood up from her chair. "So this is the path you've chosen? First, you pushed Marissa away, and now, me?"

"Goodbye, Vanessa."

"You're just going to dismiss me like that?! Like I'm some common piece of rubbish?! Is that how you do business?!" Vanessa spat. When Markus opened his mouth to respond, Vanessa placed both her hands up and closed her eyes.

"I can't even talk to you right now. Not even so much as a thank you?" Vanessa seethed, starting to walk toward the door. After a few steps, she stopped. "And another thing: When you're not busy, maybe you could construct something for my face that's a little sturdier? Make it a little less about being sexy, and a little more about … I don't know, surviving the night?"

Vanessa walked past him and went downstairs, violently slamming the door behind her. Markus sighed, laid back into the couch and looked at the ceiling. He took a few deep breaths and closed his eyes. The sun was starting to rise. He grabbed the remote off the table and pushed a few buttons. The windows in his house darkened.

"What did you do?" he muttered to himself.

He cautiously made his way back to the refrigerator, grabbing another container of his green concoction. He guzzled it and tossed the container in the sink and placed his hands on the counter.

I need her. I don't know why I did that, he thought.

There was a knock at the door. Markus felt like it took him forever to get over there once he did. He looked in the peephole. *What the hell,* he thought to himself. He cracked the door open and stood behind it. She slipped in. He closed the door behind her.

"Marissa," he said.

"I would think you'd have a little more pep in your voice when y– …" she looked him up and down. "Jesus Christ, Markus!"

She delicately touched his face. He winced and turned his head. When he turned it back, her hand was waiting. She traced the bruises on his face and looked at him.

She said, "You're a mess. Your face, your suit, you're just … a mess."

"That's part of the job," he said.

"Not like this." She scanned his body again. "Are you hurt anywhere else?"

"Yeah, everywhere. I'll be fine. No big deal."

She pushed on. "Yes it is. Where have you been the past few days? I called and called, and … nothing. You weren't at the office or answering your phone."

"I haven't checked my phone," Markus said. "I just got home. Literally just came through the door, had a conversation with Vanessa, had a little to eat, and … here we are."

She pointed at his face. "Who did that to you?"

"Police officers, the Broken Skull … if you'd like, I could pinpoint who did what, if that would make you happy."

"Don't be like that. I haven't talked to you in like, forever, so I don't need your attitude. I worry about you. We may not be an item, but we're still friends, so … this is me being a friend, in the neighborhood, checking on my friend. Do you need to sit?"

"I don't need to sit."

"Do you need help over to the couch?"

"No," Markus muttered.

"Are you going downstairs to sit in your recovery thingie?" she asked him.

"That's where I was headed before you knocked," he said. "What do you need from me, Marissa? I'll be back out on the street in less than 24 hours, and I'm tired."

Markus grimaced, clutched his side, and took a deep breath. They looked at each other for a moment, but Markus clearly wasn't in the mood to keep the conversation going. He headed toward the basement.

"I'm going downstairs with you," Marissa notified.

His eyebrows dropped in confusion. "You don't need to. I won't talk to you."

"You won't have to. Now, let me help you, and stop being such a Negative Nancy."

Marissa let Markus snake his arm around her neck.

"Is this okay?" she asked. He nodded yes.

They both walked through the basement door and rode down the platform to the ground level. He started to unzip his suit.

"Let me get that for you."

She took the reins, using her thumb and forefinger to slowly unzip his suit. As she moved the zipper down past his chest, she noticed all the bruises and welts splattered across his body. She didn't know much about pain, but she had a hunch it wasn't a one-time altercation.

She circled behind him and grabbed the shoulders of his suit. He carefully wiggled his way out. She circled back around and faced him.

He pointed with his thumb toward the door that housed the Recovery Chamber. "Okay, well … I'm going to go in–"

"Yeah. I just want you to know that I … I-I'll be here when you get out … get better … I don't really know what you call it. I'll just be here, reading a magazine. Do you have magazines in there?"

"No."

"I'll just read on my phone, then. Sweet dreams … you know, if you sleep."

They nodded at each other and went their separate ways - Markus, to the Recovery Chamber, and Marissa, to the extra room. There was nowhere to sit, just multiple workout stations. The buzz from her phone got her attention. A text, from her father.

Where are you?

Out and about. Do you need me to pick up something?

You're not with him are you?

No. I said I'm out and about. Remember?

When are you coming back to the house?

When I'm done with work. What. Do. You. Need.

Just checking on my daughter that's all.

I have to go to a meeting. Closing a deal. TTYL

No response. Her father was serious about business. With that involved, she knew Michael would stay quiet, for fear of being a distraction to his daughter's work.

On the other side of the wall, she heard the machine's faint, soothing hum. She walked to the wall and rested against it, slowly lowering herself. The machine's vibrations came through the wall and worked up and down her back. Not enough for a massage, but enough to make her feel close to him while he rested. She opened up a few apps on her phone and browsed.

It might be a while, she thought.

Jasper walked through the door of his house. He had cuts to tend to, but the distraction of the aggressive mental replay clouded his actions. He clutched his head with both hands, the tips of his fingers digging in. His palms squeezed his temples.

He knew the squeezing wouldn't help, but the visual of a dazed Vanessa remained etched in his mind. He was convinced his mind was playing tricks. He clutched his head tighter and closed his eyes.

"Stop it … stop it … stop it!" he yelled. Exasperated, he gritted his teeth.

He walked down the hallway, into the bathroom. He flipped the light on. Staring into the mirror, Jasper slowly peeled his hands off his head and turned on the faucet, cupping his hands underneath the sink. He dipped his head and smacked his face with the cold water, watching it run off his face. He ran his hands down his face, wiping off the excess water.

"I have to kill her."

17

He smacked his face again with water.

"I love her. She needs to know that."

He dried off, pulled his phone out of his pocket and punched a few keys.

Vanessa?

A few seconds later, his phone buzzed.

Hello Jasper.

I was just worried about you. Can we meet somewhere public?

That would be a safer bet, yes.

Crooked Tree in 45 minutes?

That would be okay for me. See you.

Sure. I love you.

No response.

He didn't want to send another text after he'd just professed his love for her. Instead, he busied himself by showering and cleaning himself up. He saw his reflection in the mirror, surrounded by steam and moisture. It presented a warped reflection of him, somewhat. The cuts he earned mixing it up with The Sound and Vanessa dried up. He decided against Band-Aids; they would be all over his face. The shower worked, for now.

Jasper's heart raced when he pulled up to the Crooked Tree. Breathing exercises only calmed him so much, especially with an unavoidable conflict on the horizon. With a mask on, conflicts weren't a problem. This was different.

He walked through the coffee shop doors and eventually found Vanessa sitting in the back of the shop.

With one look at her, Jasper was instantly overcome with guilt. The bruise where he'd struck her the night before still looked fresh and painful.

Without a word, he sat down. His hand moved toward hers, but he pulled it back and hid it under the table. Her look confirmed he made the right decision. He turned in his chair and crossed his legs, resting his intertwined fingers on his top knee.

"So … now that we know each other's identities, why don't we get on with it, then?" Vanessa questioned.

Jasper painted genuine confusion on his face. "Get on with what?"

"Well, why don't you take one more look at my face, and then tell me what we should get on with, huh?" she said. "I know who you are, you know who I am, so … we need to get on with it."

Jasper nodded yes. "Where do you want me to start?" he asked.

Contempt in her voice, she said, "Anywhere. Literally anywhere will do."

"Vanessa, I didn't know it was you until your mask got knocked off."

"Right, when you punched it off, you mean?" she asked.

"I don't want to dwell on that," Jasper said.

"Oh, I believe we've gone too far for your preferences," Vanessa said sternly. "If my mask hadn't shattered, you would've killed me. If I wasn't there last night, you would've killed The Sound. Can we just agree on that and move on?"

"Yes," he said quickly. He shook his head in frustration. "I just want to say I'm sor–"

She cut him off. "Don't." She leaned in and whispered, "It's not about you hitting me. I can take the hits. It's about killing people, Jasper. If you really want to say you're sorry, then stop doing what you're doing. It's that simple, really."

Vanessa felt like Jasper was looking through her. She blinked and looked harder at him. He cocked his head up and looked down on her, as if skeptical of her words.

"You remember when you and your people kidnapped me, and you injected me with something?"

"Yes, I do."

"What was it?"

His pointed chin put him eye-to-eye with her again. "Long story short, it makes people tell the truth … unless they have the fortitude to resist, like you did. Actually, you're the only one that's responded like that when injected."

More silence between them.

"I don't want to, but I feel like I'm about to lose you," he said to her.

"A relationship between us is not in the cards, especially since you almost killed me and my partner."

Jasper's lips curved on one side.

"What would you say if I told you we could both stop right now and move on with our lives?" she asked him.

"I didn't paint you as someone who would go to those depths for me," Jasper said.

"What, no one's ever loved you?" Vanessa asked. "There's got to be someone in your world that's loved you. Is that not true?"

Jasper laughed quietly. "I don't believe so, in all my years. I've been called emotionally unavailable before. A few times, actually. It's nothing I'm proud of."

"Well, I know who you are," Vanessa said. "I'm not trying to control your life. I'm just asking you to make a change, for us."

Jasper looked down. Vanessa slowly extended one of her hands to touch his. It landed on top of his intertwined hands. He slowly started to pull away.

"It's all right … it's all right," she coaxed, applying more pressure on his hand.

He moved his hand back to its prior position and glared at Vanessa.

"I like who I am."

His comment made the hairs on her arm stand at attention. Although she was visibly thrown-off by his comment, she remained undeterred.

"Then I can't, in good conscience, leave this be," she said.

He opened his hands and used one of them to take her hand. His thumb rubbed the top of her hand while she gripped his.

"I know you can't," Jasper said, "but it won't be easy."

"Someone told me something once," Vanessa said. "It wouldn't be worth it if it was easy."

"Definitely make sure that person stays around in your life. If they keep feeding you that kind of wisdom, they're definitely worth the time."

"I plan to," Vanessa said. "So … this is goodbye," she said assertively.

"It is," Jasper said. "I just don't see it going how you or I want it to go."

"Right, then."

She stood up from the table. So did he. Their hands were still involved while they stood together. Busted up, bruised – and formerly bloody – they managed to stand in the same room and be civil. About as civil as they could be in public.

He embraced her. She reciprocated the act, holding him just as tight. He leaned into her ear.

"Now that this is what it is … next time, I won't go so easy on you."

Vanessa smiled. Chuckled, even. She whispered back, "Looking forward to it."

While they were still locked in an embrace, she pulled back and faced him. For a moment, it didn't matter that they'd gotten into a fistfight the night before. It didn't matter that the next time they crossed paths, there would be violence. It was in that moment she understood that it was over, and it was for the best.

She leaned in, her lips barely touching his. She felt his breath on her bottom lip. She felt like he was holding part of himself back. She wouldn't let him. She leaned in an inch more. Their lips touched fully. She felt him kiss her back. Her heart broke more.

He finally pulled back again. His forehead rested on hers. His head slid to the side and he kissed her sweetly on the cheek before leaving the coffee shop. Vanessa stood alone, in a room full of people.

I need to get out of here, she thought. She waited for a minute or two before she left the shop and entered her car. After she shut the door and pulled her phone out to send out a text, she peered at her lock screen, a selfie of her and Jasper. She leaned her driver's seat back a few inches and looked outside through the top of the car's windshield.

She hoped to cross paths with Jasper again. Maybe when they weren't in their full night garb, but the timing would have to be better than the two of them nearly killing each other.

As one door shut, another opened.

"I've been texting and calling you forever. Are you trying to avoid me?" she asked, her head down.

"No, I'm just … do you want to come in?" he asked.

"Yes I do. I missed you."

Jonathan let Emma into his apartment and shut the door. By the time he turned back to face her, she was staring at him. He touched the various nicks on his face and shook his head. He knew what was coming.

"What happened?" she asked flatly.

"Fell."

She laughed. "Nobody falls like that." She traced his jaw. "I should know, I've seen my brother hit people. I know what those welts and nicks look like. Would you like to try again?"

"It was De La Rosa and her people, but she didn't do anything," Jon confessed.

"She just ordered it, right?" Emma said. "That's what she comes off like, to me - very bossy. Likes to let people know she's in charge, keep her hands clean."

"Yeah. She ordered it."

"Good. Now I can kill her," Emma said. "Never liked her, anyway."

She shrugged and walked toward the door.

Jon placed his hand on her shoulder. "Wait."

She turned and faced him again. "Don't. You didn't text me back, you didn't call me back. Your face is messed up, your body could be worse, for all I know. What I do know is that she's going to pay for this. You have the badge numbers or names for those officers that were with her?"

"No … that is, I don't remember," Jon said. "Emma, this is all going so fast. Please don't do this."

"So, you're going to make me go to that precinct and mow through everyone until I find who I'm looking for? Would you prefer that?" she asked.

"No! I– … just wait, okay? I don't want that on my conscience for the rest of my life. Plus, it makes us no better than them."

"You still love her, don't you?" Emma asked. She shook her head yes. "Yeah, that's what it is."

"You don't understand. I–"

"No, I do. You still love her. There's nothing else to understand."

"You need to understand the repercussions of these actions," Jon argued. "This is the entire police force we're talking about, Emma. Not some two-bit punk that needs to be roughed up. So just … just let me think."

She threw her hands up and shook her head yes.

"Okay. You think, I'll act. Sound good?"

She passed him up.

"Are you really going through with this?!" Jon asked.

She stopped. "I'm not really thinking so much as, going to," she corrected. Look, if I tell you some things, you're not going to freak out, right?" she asked.

"No, no way. I'm not going to freak out," he said.

"Okay. Good. While Patrick and I are twins, I consider him my big brother," she started, her voice almost a whisper. She looked at the floor. "When we were younger, Patrick took care of the things like this. Emotionally? Psychologically? That's more me. But I'm not just a talker, you know. I'm not afraid to get my hands dirty."

She smiled at him.

"You don't have to prove anything to me," Jon said.

"Yes, I do," she told him. "I've done a lot of bad things in my life, so none of this is new to me. I understand it's new to you. This is something I can help you with. Also, I like you. People do things for people they like. Can I go now?"

Jon tried not to blush. "You like me?"

Emma smirked. "You already knew that, silly."

She closed the door. Jon sat on the couch and flipped the TV on, already stuck in thought.

There's no way I can let her do that by herself. Well, she has her brother with her, right? I mean … I'd just get in the way and get myself killed.

He didn't want to be involved in what Emma was talking about doing. In the back of his mind, however, he felt like he'd end up hearing about it through a third party.

Like the late-night news.

18

Marissa woke up to the tick-tick sound of a keyboard. She looked around the room. The lights were still on. She looked down. Her phone sat in her hand, just barely. She turned her head to the right. All the garage lights were on. She pulled herself to her feet and walked into the open area, where Markus looked hard at work. She checked the time. She'd been sleeping three hours.

She rubbed her eyes to focus. "I see you're feeling much better, since you're up and around."

Without looking up, Markus said, "I feel as good as I'm going to feel."

"I know this is totally backwards, but … do you want to go to lunch?" she wondered.

Markus stopped typing. "Why's that backwards?" he asked, resuming his frantic typing. "Anyway, I should be ready in 30 minutes, but I'm not sure."

"Because of work?" she asked, pointing at the screen. "Or *work*?" she added, clenching her fist and showing it to him.

"The second one," Markus confessed.

"Markus … talk to me."

Markus stopped what he was doing, his eyes settling on Marissa. He shoved his hands in his robe's pockets.

179

"The Broken Skull almost killed me last night."

Marissa's eyes flashed wide. "Never mind the theatrics. Are-are … are you okay?" she asked, cautious not to overreact further.

"I think I'm okay," Markus replied. "He's stronger than anyone I've ever encountered. Like, savagely strong. Do you understand what I'm saying?"

"Yeah, like … ungodly strong, right?" she asked.

"Yes. He overpowered me pretty easily. He put his hands around my throat and just … he tried to choke me to death," Markus continued. "I looked in his eyes, just to see if I could get a read on him, something."

"What'd you get?" Marissa asked.

"Nothing."

"Like, you couldn't get a read?"

"No. There was nothing in his eyes. No anger. It was just … nothing. His grip got tighter. He didn't clench his jaw, he didn't flex. No matter how much I fought, his grip never changed."

"Why'd he stop?" she asked.

"Vanessa fought him off me," he recalled. "Got her mask cracked for her trouble. He almost killed her, too."

"What stopped him?" she asked.

"He heard sirens. Ran away."

Markus felt bad for lying, but the less Marissa knew, the better.

"I mean, in terms of fighting against someone, is this the worst it's ever been?" she asked.

"What do you mean?" Markus asked. "It's always bad."

"Yes, but is this the worst thing that's happened to you while in your suit?" she asked.

"Yes. I've never been that close to death before."

He sipped from a coffee mug with one hand, leaving his other hand in his robe. Marissa shook her head no.

"You're not done, are you?" she asked him. "Just tell me the truth."

"No."

"I wonder when it'll be enough," Marissa said. "All of this. Like, if you stop the Broken Skull, if what you have to give to the city will ever be enough. It's not like this city has really embraced you. It's not like they've been enthusiastic – or thankful – for what you've done."

"Mare …"

"I'm not saying you should stop," she interrupted, putting her hands up submissively. "I've learned my lesson with that. I'm not telling you to stop. I know Vanessa's your sidekick, but you need other people. I don't think it's healthy to internalize all this. Let me be your therapist, or something."

The last one almost killed me, Markus thought.

"Look, before you answer, I know that … you know, maybe the ship has sailed on us as a couple. I don't know what you're thinking, and I don't want to drill you, after such a hectic night. I just miss being around you every once in a while."

She very carefully wrapped her arms around his waist. He put his mug down on his work table and used that arm to wrap around her body. He pulled his other hand out of his robe pocket and wrapped that arm around her as well.

"I was scared," Markus told her. "That's never happened. Doesn't do a whole lot of good with what I do, but … I don't know. I just froze."

"What was going through your mind?" Marissa asked.

"I was about to lose everything that mattered," he responded. "Money can be recouped, but losing Vanessa, my impact on the world, and you … well, that was a hard pill to swallow."

Marissa averted her gaze from Markus as silence washed across the garage. If she looked at him, she would surely break down. From the moment she found out he was The Sound, the thought of losing him frequently haunted her thoughts. She thought he'd been shaken deep inside his soul to open up without prompt. She decided to enjoy the breakthrough moment.

"So, I don't want the ship to sail," Markus said. "Being me, it's hard for me to admit when I need help. I also don't know if you and I fit as 'just friends' anymore."

Butterflies fluttered around Marissa's stomach. She was still hesitant to look him in the eye, however. He'd pushed her away before, abandoned her.

Without looking at him, she said, "I don't think we fit as 'just friends' either, but I'm not ready for what I think you're proposing. I-I … I just don't want to be looked at as some girl you just … pick up when you need the extra support, and put down when you're feeling confident again. I don't like the yank-around."

She looked up for less than a second, and then looked back down.

"I want to be there for you, Markus. I never stopped loving you, never stopped being in love with you, but I'm not an 'on-again, off-again' type of girl. You know that. So we're going to have to work at this. Everything went too fast. I think we - well, I - was in a rush to get here and start this perfect life with you. When I found out just how imperfect it was, I panicked."

"I panicked too."

"We panicked," she corrected. "So what do we do?"

"I can't take the next step with you without making a tremendous sacrifice," he said. "I just can't stop what I'm doing."

"And I'm okay with that, but ..." she hesitated for a moment, collected her thoughts and said, "I think we're both going to have to let go of the idea of a relationship if you can't stop being The Sound."

"I hate to lose, Mare."

"Well, Markus, it's like a draw: We both lose."

"I understand," he said.

"I want everyone to come out of this alive," she told him. "Be careful."

She left his side and journeyed back upstairs. Markus looked up at the large screen above him, watched it fill up with every keystroke when he resumed typing.

Jasper typed away at his keyboard when he heard a knock at his door.

"Come in," he called from his desk.

In walked Emma. She closed the door and scurried into the chair across from him.

He intertwined his fingers and rested his hands on the desk. "What can I do for you?"

"You know I wouldn't normally come here unless it was urgent. I apologize."

"Don't worry about an apology," Jasper said. "What's the problem?"

"I need a huge favor from you."

"It must be important."

"To me, it is. I want to get Daphne De La Rosa."

Jasper's eyebrows dropped. "Can I ask what this is about?"

"You know the Deadmarsh boy?" she asked.

"I'm familiar," Jasper responded.

"I've been seeing him."

Jasper leaned back in his chair and huffed out a laugh. He pointed at Emma.

"You mean to tell me … we've been terrorizing a guy that has you all wrapped up?" he questioned. "Never mind how it happened. I find it all just … fascinating."

Emma smiled. "He didn't have me wrapped up from the beginning. I don't know … something just happened. He's actually a really nice guy."

"I believe you. Now, what do you mean about wanting to get De La Rosa?"

"He was jailed. She was the reason. We have morals, Jasper. People may not understand everything we do, but there's a method to it. I believe she's using him to get information. He doesn't see it, but she's making it more and more dangerous for him, with every interaction."

"So … where do I come in?" Jasper asked.

"You can draw her out," Emma said. "We don't need to kill her, but a message should be sent."

"You feel strongly about this," Jasper told her. "If you feel it's worth it, you have my support."

A big and wide smile took up most of Emma's face. She nodded her head yes and placed one of her hands atop Jasper's.

"I knew I came to the right person."

"That's what family is for," he said. "Tonight is the night, then."

"Most definitely. I'll make sure Patrick is ready."

The night saw Patrick and Emma posted up at the end of a street. Patrick studied the crumpled piece of paper in his hand, then passed it to Emma.

"Is this the right address?" he asked, skeptically shrugging. "I know Jasper's been around here a time or two, but I'm not too familiar with this part of town."

Emma looked at the scribble and gave him a quick, positive nod. They started their walk down the street.

"Nice night for a stroll, wouldn't you say?" he asked.

"I *would* say," she agreed.

While the two walked down the street, they pulled leather gloves onto their hands, opening and closing their fingers to make sure they were snug. Emma locked arms with Patrick, maintaining the same stride until they got to the front door of the address written on the paper.

"Who are we tonight?" Patrick asked.

"Ummm … let's just be us. You okay with that?" Emma suggested.

"I've been wanting to be myself for a while." Patrick grinned at his counterpart, knocking on the door.

"Coming!" they heard. A few seconds later, De La Rosa opened up the door. She frowned at the two, pushing the door a few inches back toward them and splitting her body between the door and frame.

"What do you want?" she asked.

Patrick raised his eyebrows. "We're ummm … here to deliver a message? You look a lot different when you're not doing prostitution stings, you know that?"

De La Rosa's eyes tightened. She looked back and forth between them. They looked back at her. Without warning, she shut the door. Patrick's forearm blocked it. She pushed with her shoulder, trapping his arm.

He swiped at her face, trying to grab for something, anything. A couple of his fingernails nicked her jaw. In that short moment she let up, she found herself overpowered by the force of the twins. She backed away. They barged in, crossing the threshold.

"It's just business. Come quietly, or this could end badly," Patrick said to the detective, holding his arm while Emma locked the door.

"I think this might have to end badly," De La Rosa warned.

Patrick grabbed the detective, threw her onto the couch and pounced. He tried to grab hold of her wrists. She clawed his eyes, feeling his skin break against her slow-moving fingernails. He backed off. She positioned herself between the two aggressors and the coffee table.

"Come quietly," Patrick repeated.

"I told you it was the second one!" she exclaimed, kicking him in the knee. It buckled underneath him. He fell to the floor, inadvertently blocking the front door. Daphne turned to find another way out. Patrick grabbed her foot. With her free foot, she kicked him in the face. He rolled over and writhed in pain.

"I'm not Deadmarsh," Daphne bitterly mocked. She leapt on Patrick and punched wildly, striking his face and neck. She felt his struggle; he wasn't small, yet he was having a great amount of trouble getting her off him.

Emma finally snapped out of it and grabbed Daphne from behind. The detective reared back and smashed Emma's face with the back of her head. Emma immediately screamed out, cupping her hands under her nose as blood poured out.

De La Rosa stood up, leaving Patrick on the ground. She then shoved Emma to the ground, right by her brother.

"You didn't see that coming, did you?!" she asked the two.

While she reveled in her victory, less than a second elapsed between her feeling the grip on her hair, the downward-jerking motion, and the back of her head smash onto the living room floor. The carpet softened the blow, but only so much.

De La Rosa slowly ran her fingers along the back of her head. She felt like her skull was cracked open. Everything was fuzzy. The Broken Skull snatched a fistful of her t-shirt, pulling her to her feet.

"You want to fight for your life?" he asked the detective. She didn't answer. Her legs were still wobbly. He pulled her close.

"I don't believe you're the type, but … if you even think about screaming … I'll beat you to death." His forehead grinded against hers. "I love a good game of Cat and Mouse, but here's a game for you. Do you know what it's called?"

She didn't answer.

"It's called … how many …"

He punched her.

"Punches …"

Again.

"Will it take?"

He punched her one more time. Her t-shirt's fabric slipped through his fingers. Her body dropped by his side, her face, a bloody mess. He shook his hand out.

"She's had enough … for now." He placed his fingers under De La Rosa's nostrils for a moment. "She's still alive." He looked up at the twins, who'd gathered themselves by the door.

"This is what family does for each other," the Broken Skull said. "For the Cause."

"For the Cause," the twins said in unison.

19

Jon found himself on the other side of town.

"Okay, drive slow, see if anyone's there. If she's there, stop and chat. Well, *maybe* stop and chat. She doesn't deserve it, but I deserve an explanation," he reasoned in his head. His SUV slowly crept by De La Rosa's house. The door was wide open. He parked along the curb and jumped out.

"Looks like a late night," he laughed quietly to himself.

A mess on the carpet set his senses on fire as he approached. He jogged to the front door and stepped one foot inside. The coffee table was knocked over, the couch pillow cushions were all over the place, and worse: Blood on the floor.

"Holy …"

Look around, Jon. His eyes repeatedly scanned the living room. He was trapped; he couldn't go into the other rooms. The last thing he wanted was to appear involved with whatever happened. Jon found a roundish, shallow, head-shaped blood puddle. The carpet looked tampered with.

"Jesus. I need to …"

He dug deep in his mind to recall the number he dialed when he and Leonard were picked up from captivity. When he found the number to dial, he pushed Send and held his ear to the receiver.

"We have no more business," the voice on the other side said.

"Wait!" Jon pleaded. It was too late. They hung up on him. He pushed a few buttons and held the phone to his ear again.

"Listen closely. You need to forget this number. Now," the voice on the other end snapped.

"Please … hold on. Please, just … give me one second to explain something," Jon said.

"Go."

"They took her."

"Who is 'They', who is 'Her?' and why do I care?" the voice asked.

"I have an idea of who did it. Can we meet somewhere? Please?"

"For all I know, this could be another set-up. That's how you got The Sound, after all."

"I don't know how I can prove it to you. I don't. I just …"

"Should call the police?"

"If it were that easy, I would've already done that. I don't trust them."

"And you trust me? Good Lord, your priorities are all-to-cock."

"Please … I'll do anything. You can't turn down the Superhero Code. You can't. No matter what you feel about me, just … I don't know what to do or who else to call. Please."

"All right. Stop groveling. I'm not able to help you, but I have a friend who can. Be in the alleyway behind Coleman's tonight, around 1 A.M."

"Oh my God. Thank you so much. I– … Hello?"

Dead air. It would be 1 A.M. in about an hour and a half. He sent a text to Emma.

Hey. What are you up to?

Ooh not much. You?

Not much. Too busy to hang out, maybe?

Not tonight. I'm tired. Raincheck?

Yeah, I guess.

Don't pout. We'll have fun. You should be sleeping anyway!

I know. Just can't sleep.

Drink some warm milk. Helps me sleep. Goodnight, Mister.

Goodnight.

After a long drive to clear his thoughts, Jon landed in the back alley of Coleman's, a very popular restaurant in the city. It had been closed for a few hours already, the alley was quiet as could be. He checked his watch. One after 1.

Feet slammed against the pavement. Jon jumped and turned to face the voice.

"Sorry so late."

Pale-faced, he clutched his chest and said, "No, it's okay. I might've died a little, but it's okay."

"Okay, I'm here, and so is he. What do you want?"

Jon looked up at the fire escape. The Sound was just making his way down.

Jon directed his eyes to The Sound. "Okay, first of all, I'm sorry for the–"

"Not what we came here for," the Ivory Fox interrupted.

"She's right," The Sound said. "What do you need?"

"They took De La Rosa."

The Ivory Fox laughed and started to walk away. Jon put his hands at his waist and sighed, shook his head. Before he had a chance to say anything, the Ivory Fox turned around and approached him again.

The Fox pointed to her chest. "You think I care if someone took her?" she questioned. "Couldn't care less. Good riddance, I say. She's been shooting at us for a good while now. She almost killed me." She pointed at The Sound. "She almost killed him." She pointed at Jon. "She's almost killed *you*! She's just getting what's coming to her. Serves her right."

She turned and walked away again. After a few steps, she stopped. She looked at The Sound.

"Are you coming? Please tell me you're not entertaining this madness."

The Sound did what he did best: Said nothing.

"Oh, for the love of God." Ivory Fox turned again and kept walking.

The Sound asked Jon, "Who is 'they'?"

"I think it was the Broken Skull, maybe some other people."

The Fox stopped, turned around, and approached him again.

"What'd you say?" she asked him.

"I said I think the Broken Skull did this," Jon echoed. "Remember when he broke into her house? He had an opportunity to kill her then, but didn't. He's like a spider: Gets you trapped in his web, toys with you until he kills you. If I were still a detective, he's my number one suspect."

"We'll be with you in a moment."

The Sound walked over to the Fox. They both turned their back to Jon.

"That's a lot of information," he said to her. "We need to find a way to get her back."

"I'm sorry … *we?!*" she whispered loudly. "This is not our fight!"

"As soon as he said something about the Broken Skull, it became our fight," The Sound said. "Actually, it became more your fight."

"Everything's going way too fast. Explain this," she said.

"It's simple: You're in—"

"Were."

"You were in a relationship with him. Between you and I, you have the best odds of reasoning with him without violence happening. Plus, you can move anonymously. I can't."

The Fox sighed.

"Peace first, right? Isn't that what we're going for?"

"All right, just shut up about it, okay? Bollocks."

She walked back over to Jon and muttered, "We'll help you. And because you owe him," she said, pointing to The Sound, "that means you need to tell us everything you know. Right now."

Jon visibly hesitated, stumbled over some inaudible words.

"The truth. Now," she said.

Jon placed his hands out in defeat. "I don't know much. The Broken Skull have a brother and sister combo that work with him, Patrick and Emma Starks. They're dangerous. Emma said she wanted to go after De La Rosa. That's really the only lead I have."

"How do you know Emma said that?" Ivory Fox asked.

"I heard it, first-hand."

"How do you know her?"

"We've ummm ... we've seen each other, here and there."

"Lord, help us," she blurted out, immediately after Jon answered. "So, you're directly involved with her. That's how you know so much."

"Yes."

"Do you know anything else about them, besides maybe what Emma's bed looks like?" she asked. She looked over at The Sound. He simply shook his head.

"I know Patrick works at the casino. Emma's unemployed."

"We'll take it from here."

The Fox walked away. The Sound nodded and followed. As they walked down the alley, he looked at the Fox and said, "Nice touch. So, how are you going to play this?" he asked.

"How am I? You want me to plan this whole thing out?" she asked.

He opened his car's door. "You need to take the lead on this, yes."

She straddled her bike. "Might as well start at the casino."

"Good thinking. That's exactly what I'd do."

She started her bike. He started his car. They both sped off in different directions.

A few hours later, Vanessa entered the casino, dressed in plain clothes. She eventually was able to confirm that Jon wasn't lying - Patrick Starks was there. She didn't know the layout of the casino, outside what the computer was able to pull up. This one wasn't a run-of-the-mill casino; this was the one to be at.

She tried her best to hide her nervousness. She knew Markus would support her when the chips were down. She also knew she needed to show she could handle something on her own.

She took in the atmosphere as she toured the casino. It wasn't as alive as it would be around midnight, with a few stragglers here and there. She looked down and grimaced a little.

Jeans, jacket, and t-shirt. Once again, underdressed for the occasion. Hopefully, they don't mind.

A waiter passed by.

"Excuse me. Can you point me to the security room?" she asked the man.

"Yes, it's—"

The waiter narrowed his eyes at Vanessa. "Is there something I can help you with?"

"Oh, I'm sorry. I should've clarified. I'm here to fix a monitor," she said.

He looked at her hands. "You don't have any tools with you."

She looked down, and then back up. With a smile, she said, "I just need to re-wire some things. Don't really need tools for that."

"Maybe you can re-wire some things for me sometime. I get off in about two hours," he told her.

"I like a man that cuts to the chase. I think we can make something happen, but I need you to do something for me. Security guard … I think his name is Patrick, something like that?" she asked, raising her eyebrows like she didn't know.

"Oh, Patty?" the waiter said, nodding his head. "I think he's about to come back from his lunch break." He checked his watch. "Yeah, he'll be back on the clock in around 5 minutes."

"Send him up when you see him, would you?" she requested. "I know he's on the monitors a lot, so I wanted to make sure it was nice and clear for him."

"Definitely," he said. "And here."

The waiter scribbled on a napkin and handed it to Vanessa. He then pointed her in the direction of the control room. They exchanged smiles before Vanessa turned on her heel and headed toward the room.

Whatever it takes, even if it means getting a number from a slimebucket.

She walked up the flight of stairs and down a short hallway before she found the room.

"Authorized Personnel," she recited out loud. She was authorized enough. She entered the spacious room with a few minutes to kill. The first thing she did was throw that pesky waiter's scribbled-on napkin in the trash.

"I wonder what this button does?" she asked herself, hovering her finger over the button. "Surely, things will go wrong if I start hitting buttons," she added, laughing.

She took a seat and waited, checking her watch again. A couple minutes later, the door opened. With his head down, a man walked in. When he turned and saw Vanessa, he froze. Vanessa noticed various cuts and scrapes on the man's face. She also noticed that when he reached for the door to close it, he winced, then used his other hand. It struck her as odd.

"Oh, can I help you with something?" he asked plainly.

"You sure can," she said, leaning back in the chair. "Patrick, right?"

He smiled. "Yeah. Patrick."

"Well, looks like I'm in the right place. I'm looking for detective De La Rosa. A little birdie told me you know where she is."

Patrick shook his head incredulously.

"I know who you are. We should've killed you. I told him, but he didn't listen."

So much for that mask harboring my identity, Vanessa thought.

"So, I guess it's up to me." Patrick walked over and locked the door. With one hand, he grabbed his chin and cracked his neck. "So, do you need to stretch or warm up?"

Vanessa stood up. "Nope. I'm afraid I've already done all that. What about you? Do you need to pray to your deity of choice?"

"No. I'm ready," he said simply. He wrung his hands out and loosened them up.

"Okay, well–"

Vanessa charged Patrick, clocked him quick. He staggered back, the door stopping his momentum. She threw punches to his face and body with ferocity. He absorbed every one and pushed her away. She charged him again. He popped her in the face, knocking her to the ground.

Vanessa sat up. Her faculties could catch up later. Patrick ran and kicked at her face. She flattened out, straight as a plank. His foot just missed its mark. Before he could turn to face her, she scrambled to her feet and buried her fist in his ribs as hard as she could. His body deflated. He grabbed her to keep from falling. He reared back and punched her with his bad arm. She threw another heavy body blow. She felt his breath hit her shirt.

In a fit of desperation, he lifted her up by the jacket and tossed her on top of the room's control board. She landed hard and rolled to the ground. She looked up as he approached. He kicked her in the ribs. She rolled to her side. He squatted and scooped her limp body up by the lapels of her jacket.

"Probably not the outcome you hoped for," Patrick said.

Vanessa's arms came alive. She snaked an arm around the back of his neck, held him close, and bit him. He screamed, frantically pushing her away, but her teeth stayed locked. Her hands latched on to his ears. She unhinged her jaw, reared back and head-butted him.

He dropped her. She got back to work, chopping him down with each body blow. He attempted to punch her again, but the body blows proved too much.

He threw a punch. She hooked his arm, then smashed the side of his head with her other forearm. The force sent him sprawling over her hips and onto the ground. She straddled his back, locking him in a chokehold. She yelled loudly while she flexed her arm. Patrick let out a high-pitched squeal. She arched her back to get more leverage.

She felt like she was sitting atop a volcano. She heard him struggling underneath her, so she squeezed harder. He lifted his hips. She lost control. She'd exerted most of her energy holding him down.

She wasn't completely to her feet. Patrick charged again. She threw a haymaker to stop him. Too late. He drove her back. The momentum was too much to stop. The tackle took the two over the control board and through the security room's window.

Thinking quickly, she put all her energy into turning her hips. She locked her free arm over one of his arms and pulled.

They landed. The thud of the shattered roulette table rocked the casino. Everything in the casino stopped. Through the quiet, no one moved. Finally, Vanessa lazily rolled over to her back. Her body heaved up and down. She slowly opened her eyes, peering at the lights above her.

Still alive.

Vanessa's eyes flickered as she sat up gingerly. When she was able to focus, she looked over at Patrick. He was still breathing, but out cold. When she got to her feet, she scanned the room. All eyes were fixed on her, all mouths, too stunned to speak. Clearing blood from her mouth with her thumb and forefinger, she hobbled to the front door of the casino.

On her way out, she passed by the waiter that had given her his number, no more than 10 minutes ago. His eyes wide and his mouth just barely open, it looked to her like he wanted to say something. She simply nodded at him and kept moving.

20

After another tip from Jonathan Deadmarsh, Vanessa found herself at a motel right outside town. She parked her car right past the entrance. She looked down at her ribs, touched them, and winced. Though Patrick broke her fall, she still found herself in immense pain. Her wrist throbbed, her knee ached, and her neck and back were sore.

"Another day in paradise," she murmured.

She gingerly stepped out of her car and walked across the parking lot. She peered across the ruined landscape - cheap and dirty, the perfect place to lay low.

She pulled out her phone and read the number on the text message again. She repeated it in her head until her eyes landed on a beautiful distraction - one of the motel's maids, ambling along with a rolling cart of cleaning supplies. She jogged up and stopped in front of the cart, startling the middle-aged woman.

"Erm, excuse me. Are you cleaning this floor?" Vanessa asked.

"Yes," she replied. Her accent was thick.

"Okay. Room 42, that's where I'm staying. I left my keys in there accidentally, so … is there any way you could open that door up for me so I can grab them?"

The maid nodded and fiddled through her marked keys until she found the right one. The trek was short. Vanessa stayed a few steps behind. When they arrived at the room, Vanessa knelt down behind the cart.

"I'm sorry, just have to tie my shoe," she said casually.

The maid nodded again, isolated the key to the room, and slid it into the keyhole. The door ripped open.

"Don't you knock?!" Vanessa heard. Before there was an answer, the voice coldly said, "I don't care about the reason, just come in and do your job."

Vanessa barely peered out from behind the cart. Her next target walked into the bathroom. When it quieted again, she rose from behind the cart.

Vanessa faked an irritated look. "Thank you. Apologies about my friend. She's so, so rude."

When the maid scuttled away, Vanessa closed the door behind her. When she heard the toilet flush, her heart rate spiked. She took a couple deep breaths and exhaled. The door opened. Emma Starks emerged. When she saw Vanessa, she froze.

"Raise your hand if you thought I'd be standing here, waiting for you?" she asked, lightly raising her hand.

Emma raised her hand, just barely. "I knew that boy would rat me out sooner or later," she muttered, rubbing her weathered face. Her hands shook. "I honestly didn't think you'd make it. When I heard about your run-in with my brother, I thought for sure you'd be out of commission. I see you're not."

"I am not," Vanessa said.

"It would've been a better idea to leave town, see the end of this from afar," she smiled weakly.

"You know the Deadmarsh boy cares about you," Vanessa said to her. "You should've just told him you were never going to change. Instead, you keep stringing him along."

"You have *no* idea how I feel about that boy," Emma said. "And I *have* changed. De La Rosa got hers because of the way I feel about him. No other reason."

"Is she still alive?" Vanessa questioned.

"My guess is yes," Emma replied. "And I'll make it easier for you - the Broken Skull has her under wraps."

"Why are you giving up this information so easily?" Vanessa wondered. "I thought I was going to have to beat it out of you, and here you are, giving me everything."

"You're a dense one, aren't you?" Emma gibed. "I told you, I'm different now. That, and you almost killed my brother. He's in the hospital - or that's what I hear - and I'm trapped in this crappy motel. I just want to be free. He's all I have left. If this information gets me out of your crosshairs so I can see him, so be it."

Vanessa nodded. "It has." She turned and gripped the doorknob.

"You won't get through the Skull," Emma deadpanned. "He won't think twice about killing you. You're tough, but a killer? No. And you can't convince me otherwise."

"I sure would like to try," Vanessa said.

The tall brunette left the motel room. She needed to heal and think.

As one door shut, another opened.

The Broken Skull locked the door and composed himself. De La Rosa started to stir. When her eyes flickered open, he knelt down beside her.

"I believe this is where it finally dawns on you how deep this goes," he said. "I'm going to ask you one question, and based on your answer, I'm either going to hurt you, or … well, I'm going to hurt you, anyway."

He began fiddling around inside a clean, new-looking duffel bag. Small clangs as his fingers moved around the bag. He shook his head in dismay.

"I think you should think about what you're doing," De La Rosa said. "I mean, *really* think about it."

"I already did. Every time, it plays out the exact same way," he nodded. "Hopefully, by the time we're done meeting, I can deter you from ever coming after anyone with a mask. For your sake, my hope is that you see my side sooner, rather than later."

"You're going to have to come a lot stronger than just a threat," she told him. "You wouldn't have me shackled up if there wasn't any doubt. Maybe you don't know how this works."

"Tell me your plans."

She tilted her head upward again to a more natural position. "Get you and your kind off the street. The end. Nothing else."

He finally found what he was looking for inside the bag - a shiny, stainless steel scalpel. He nodded at it, mesmerized by its shine and sharpness. He rolled it between his thumb and forefinger.

"Not the best answer," he said.

21

Two days had passed.

Daphne received "special treatment" every hour. It wasn't always the scalpel, either. She was tired and disoriented; as soon as she would nod off, the Broken Skull would be back in. Still, she wouldn't give the Broken Skull any information. She imagined it was getting to him.

She also imagined he enjoyed what he was doing, regardless of how she reacted. She saw nothing when she looked in his eyes. No anger, no hate. Nothing. He seemed completely focused on her, with no end to the torture in sight.

An alarm went off. In walked the Broken Skull. She thought about two scenarios that could happen at any moment - she could break, or he could kill her. He ambled over to her side and bunched up a handful of her mussed hair.

"How are things?" he asked.

Her eyes remained closed. He let go of her hair. Her head dropped again. He rested his fingers underneath her nose. She blinked rapidly, her head swayed around, as if she was possessed. He let go of her nose and took a seat across from her.

"It's funny what your body can do if the mind is strong," he said.

She said nothing.

"You're probably hungry. I can go days, weeks without eating," he boasted. "I don't have to sleep. There's plenty of time to do what I want to you."

"You're being irrational," Daphne pushed out, her words barely traveling. "Let me go. No revenge will be in play, nothing. I'll let this go. We'll call it even."

He laughed maniacally. "Even? Detective … I don't think we'll ever be even, as long as you're hunting people wearing masks. There's no button to rewind this, no matter how badly you might want to push it."

"Yeah … you're real demented," she said through hard breaths.

"One could argue that we're all demented," he answered. He pushed his hand into his duffel bag, rummaging through it. "Oh … that's peculiar." He picked up the bag and held it upside down.

With indifference in his words, he said, "That's all, I'm afraid. Time to die."

As he approached, Daphne's body tensed up. She looked through the only eye she was able to open.

"I have some information."

The Broken Skull stopped.

"If you kill me … I promise you … as soon as the police find out what you did-"

"It won't matter," the Broken Skull interrupted. "If I kill you, things change."

Daphne's look changed. For so long, she believed the streets were better because of her approach to masked vigilantes. All she did was pull the weeds on the surface. The Broken Skull's roots were deeper than she ever imagined.

"You should have left well enough alone."

Those were his last words. He walked behind Daphne's chair, sliding his forearm across her throat, locking onto his opposite elbow. He rested his locked arm on the back of her head and squeezed.

The chokehold started the process of taking Daphne's life. Reacting to the lack of oxygen, her body tensed up. He squeezed harder and lifted up. Daphne's body convulsed. Her legs kicked. She had nothing to hold her up.

"No one will know … or care," he grunted in her ear while he squeezed. "I could crush your windpipe and watch you choke on your own blood."

Her eyes rolled into the back of her head. Her body started to relax.

"Just a little more … it will be over soon," he whispered.

The phone's buzz in his pocket was loud. He dropped her immediately. Her body crashed sideways, her head faintly cracking against the ground. Her eyes returned from behind her head. She gulped down mouthfuls of air between violent coughs.

He accepted the call.

"Where are you?"

"Just accumulating bargaining chips," the voice said on the other side of the phone. He knew who it was. "I know you have the detective, but she doesn't matter to me as much as Patrick and Emma do to you."

"Patrick was your handy work?" the Broken Skull asked.

"Afraid so," the voice said. "I need proof of life. Give De La Rosa the phone."

The Broken Skull put the receiver by the detective's mouth. "Speak."

"I don't know who this is, but–"

The Broken Skull snatched the phone away. "She's not in the greatest shape, but it could be a lot worse. Come to the house. You know the place."

"What if I don't want to?" the voice said.

"Well, I'm a man of my word. You can keep playing it tough, and listen to her die slowly."

"Go."

"Tell me … do you know why I did all this?" he asked.

"Not the slightest idea," the voice said.

"I had to know how far you'd go," he said. "However, let me remind you - you're not invincible. You just haven't run into someone that could finish the job."

"Is that really you?" she asked him. "After all we had?"

Silence on the Broken Skull's end.

"Hello?" she called.

"I'm issuing a challenge. Me and you, one for one. I win, I'll kill the detective. Should something unforeseen happen, you can have her. High stakes with a life on the line. Do we have a deal?"

"I see you're that far gone," she told him. "Listen, we're obviously at odds about the importance of someone's life. I may not like her, but I hate what you stand for," she said sternly. "So, I'll be there, if you really want to know what I'm made of. I've got to do something about you, and I'm very sorry for that."

She hung up the phone.

22

Markus exited the platform in the garage and checked his watch. He looked around. Something about the quiet darkness in the garage that made him feel at ease.

"We're a go."

His garage changed to his command center. His and Vanessa's suit racks popped up from behind the wall. Vanessa's was already gone.

A little early, he thought.

He grabbed his suit off the rack, and was still wiggling into it on his way to the computer. As he zipped his suit up, he noticed an envelope attached to the computer's keyboard. He pulled it off and opened it, unfolding the note.

Markus,

You're not home, so we're doing it this way. Listen. I know I've been making some noise over the past couple days. Sorry for that. I aimed to make you proud. That's all really. I remember you saying

212

there's a difference between heroic and reckless. I get that now.

Which is why I aim to get rid of this scumbag, for everything he's done to us but also the city.

Just so you know, you saved me that night in the hotel room. Everything has been so good since you came around. I truly can't imagine what my life would be without you. I also know this is a big no-no, but it's something you need to know. I love you. Maybe we can talk about it over coffee sometime.

Peace First,

Vanessa

P.S. Thanks for the new mask. I love it. :)

"Damn it."

Markus tossed the note onto the computer keyboard and rushed to his car. He was scrambling to put his mask on when he punched the gas. He'd fasten his seatbelt later; there was no time to lose. The mouth of his garage was still opening when he sped through it, and down the back road.

"Computer: Ivory Fox's exact location! Hurry!"

Vanessa's mouth dried in anticipation. She left her bike on the side of the road, walking up the pathway that led to the Broken Skull's house, about a mile out. The Broken Skull instructed her to meet him somewhere at a certain time, like the old Spaghetti Westerns her father liked so much.

She hopped off the path, opting to sneak through the wooded area. Vanessa wondered if sneaking naturally made people walk slower. Even though every thought ended with her wanting to rush, she decided against it. The stakes were too high.

Once she made it to the front door of the house, thoughts of her prior captivity came flooding back. She then remembered that the walk seemed longer because she wasn't in a full sprint. She smirked at the memory. She was sure her fondness for such a dangerous night wouldn't resonate the same with a normal person.

She listened for sounds coming from behind the door. Nothing.

"You're ready. You're ready. You're ready." Her short pep talk was reminiscent of when she first interviewed with Markus to be his assistant. This time around, she felt infinitely more prepared.

Seconds of tinkering was all it took to unlock the door. She barely turned the knob and slowly pushed the door open, just enough for her body to slip through.

Vanessa's eyes landed on a bound and gagged Daphne De La Rosa. One look at the detective gave Vanessa pause. She looked dingy - mussed hair and dirty clothes, with bruises plastered all over her skin. Dried blood surrounded the chair she sat in.

Must've turned tail and run, Vanessa thought. She slowly approached the detective. She noticed small, precise cuts all over her fingers and hands. She scanned upward until her eyes landed on De La Rosa's. One of the detective's eyes was swollen shut. It sounded like she was struggling to breathe.

Vanessa blinked hard. This was the work of her ex-boyfriend? She couldn't believe it, and yet, she could.

"Maybe I can untie you before anyone shows back up?" she said.

As Vanessa closed in, De La Rosa started to struggle with her shackles. It sounded like she was trying to say something, but Vanessa couldn't make it out. She narrowed her eyes.

"All right, just calm down. I'm here to help you get out of here."

Suddenly, the detective twisted her wrists this way and that. She shook in the chair she was bound to, stomping the ground over and over.

"It's fine. Everything's going to be all-right."

Then, Vanessa heard a different sound. She whipped around. There he was.

"The hero doesn't always win," the Broken Skull said to her. "Sometimes … and only sometimes … the right one comes out on top."

Vanessa thought she'd try it Markus's way.

"No hands need to be thrown. Just let her go. Do me a favor, just this once?"

"I'd love to, but I'm afraid we're too far in for a favor," the Broken Skull said.

"Right, then," she said grimly.

The Broken Skull approached. So did the Ivory Fox. Her fist connected with his jaw. He slapped both his hands on her neck and ran as hard as he could. Despite her resistance, he ran her into De La Rosa, toppling all three of them over. She hastily got to her feet. He clasped his hands around her throat again.

Their eyes met.

She still felt something for him, but that didn't matter. His gaze was empty. She popped him in the face, kneed him in the groin and pushed him away. Her chest heaved up and down. So did his.

Through short breaths, she said, "You'll have to kill me."

"You're bluffing. I know you are." His breaths were short and shallow. "You don't want to die tonight."

She stared him down. "You think I'm bluffing, do you? Why haven't you taken a step yet, then? Come and find out if I'm bluffing, will you?"

With one hand, she motioned for the Broken Skull. He didn't move. She motioned for him again - this time, with her index finger - like a parent scolding their child.

"What are you waiting for?" she asked. "C'mon."

Quick as a cat, the Broken Skull rushed, kicking her in the chest. She staggered back, worked to recover. He threw an accurate punch, same as the one on the rooftop. Instead of shattering, the mask barely budged. The force stunned her, made her legs wobble. He caught her by the collar, pulled her to her feet, and flung her against the wall. Her body crashed to the ground.

"This will be over soon," he warned as he slowly approached. The Fox rolled over to her back, shaking her head to regain her faculties. Just as he reached down to place his hands on her throat, he stopped.

De La Rosa screamed so loud, it bordered on banshee level. Her voice broke, but she continued to scream with her entire being.

He let go of the Fox and turned toward Daphne, but was tripped up by the Fox as he moved to converge. As he scrambled to regain his balance, the Fox popped him in the back of the head. He fell down again, scrambling back to his feet.

The two were breathing shallow breaths when they faced each other.

She charged him. He threw a punch. She ducked and connected with one of her own. The Fox connected with another hard shot just as he tagged her. What was a scrum quickly became a slugfest.

The Fox connected clean on a sneaky shot that made the Skull's hands drop. Sensing a light at the end of the tunnel, she grabbed him by the turtleneck and punched away, her arm resembling a piston pumping in a car.

The Broken Skull tried backing away, but the Fox's pull was too much. His back hit a wall. Nowhere to go. The Fox punched away with all she had left. Every punch to the face and body connected now. He moved to avoid the Fox's power. The last punch she threw sent him careening out the window.

Her hands on her knees, the Fox worked on regulating her breathing. She stood upright and rested her hands on her hips. Her heavy breathing eventually subsided. She ambled over to the window sill and looked out, deep into the wooded area.

He was gone.

She pinched one side of her nostril shut and blew the contents of her nose out the other side, a mixture of blood and mucus. The glob smacked the floor and stuck. She sidestepped her mess – wiping her mouth with her glove – and pulled De La Rosa back upright in her chair. She pulled and tore at the restraints until the detective was free, and then helped her to her feet.

The Fox turned and looked at the front door.

"That may be it, unless someone comes and kicks this door down. Maybe someone tougher." She barely chuckled to herself. She turned back toward De La Rosa. "I don't-"

She froze, like she was hit with a bucket of ice-cold water. De La Rosa held the nape of the Fox's neck. The Fox opened her mouth, gasping for air. She felt like her senses had been thrown in a blender.

She looked down. The knife was nearly handle-deep. She felt De La Rosa's tight grip. She tried to grab the knife. De La Rosa pushed it deeper. Her pain sharpened. Her eyes flickered slow as she faded, her body starting to relax.

With one more attempt, the Fox used all her strength to pull away. Her hand touched the knife again, but De La Rosa's grip firmed. The more she tried to stay close, the more De La Rosa ground the knife inside her.

"He was wrong about something," De La Rosa whispered to the Fox. "I'm the hero … and I always win."

De La Rosa finally let go of the knife and shoved the Fox to the ground. She crashed to the floor in a heap. Blood started to escape the wound. Her skin hugged the knife's edges, keeping it snugly settled.

The Fox had never been so tired in her life. Just seconds ago, she was fighting to catch her breath. Right now, she didn't even want to breathe, it hurt so much. Her mind raced, the thoughts traveling like shooting stars.

Things were getting hazy.

Her eyes were open just enough to watch De La Rosa walk out of the house's front door. She slowly followed, applying hard pressure to her wound. She reached out to grab a nearby wall, but was unsuccessful. She stumbled, hitting the floor, rolling over to her back.

She turned her head to the side, the tears from one eye running straight to the floor. Her other eye dropped tears that rolled over her nose and dripped on the carpet. Finally, as if mercifully, the Ivory Fox's eyes closed.

"Faster."

The black and blue car zoomed down one of the streets and fishtailed onto another. The car gathered speed again, going down the barely-familiar dirt road that led to the house where he snatched Vanessa from the clutches of the Broken Skull.

"Proximity Check. Hurry."

The grid popped up. He scanned it quickly, two times through. One in the vicinity. In less than a minute, he was at the house. He slammed on the brakes and threw it in park. He ran to the front door and smashed it into a few fragments with one kick.

He saw her.

Vanessa, eyes closed, lying in a small pool of blood. Her suit was dirty, and her face was beat to hell.

Markus ripped his mask off.

"Vanessa?! Vanessa?! Can you hear me?!" Markus asked. He got no answer.

He noticed her chest moving. Going against everything in his heart, he pulled his mask back on, scooped her up, and jogged to his car. He used his body to open the passenger door and lightly laid her on the seat. Once he got himself in, he sped back down the road.

"I need to see the road with the least resistance! Hurry!" he commanded. After a short process, a grid popped up. He read it twice over and kept his foot glued to the gas.

"Stay with me, Vanessa. Stay with me," he directed. He looked over periodically to make sure she was still breathing while he navigated the streets. There was a sense of urgency and panic like never before. When he fought the Broken Skull, it wasn't panic. When Dwight Durant held up the restaurant, he didn't feel panic.

Vanessa was dying in front of him. He felt panic.

He found himself on the back road that led to his garage. The RPM ticker rested in the red when he pushed the accelerator all the way down to the car's floor. He was going well over 100 miles per hour. He looked over again. Vanessa's chest was still moving, but slower now.

Damn it.

The garage opened. His car shot down the ramp and down the pathway, then skidded to a stop. When he did, he placed his arm across Vanessa's chest, so her body wouldn't move around. He hurried out of the driver's seat and scooped Vanessa out.

"Don't worry. Just give me one second. One second," he said as he sprinted over to the Recovery Chamber. He dipped her body slightly so he could use his hand to pull the chamber open. He slid her in as carefully as he could and shut it. One turned switch from Markus, and the machine hastily pulled up her vital signs. A steady, slow beep filled the room.

Vanessa's eyes opened, just barely.

Markus smiled at her, nodding his head yes. "I got you here."

She smiled weakly. "I knew you would."

Tears filled her eyes. She pursed her trembling lips while tears ran down her face. Markus placed his hand on the window, the closest he could get to her while she was in the chamber.

Vanessa's hand slowly rose to meet his, landing on the chamber's window. She nodded. "It's all-right."

She closed her eyes and released a small exhale. Her arm fell down by her side. Her chest stopped moving. The slow, steady beeps that filled the room were replaced by a single steady beep.

Markus's eyes darted back and forth.

"Vanessa?!" he called, his voice smacking the chamber's window. No response. "Vanessa?!" he called again. Still no response. He balled up his fist and slammed it rapidly against the chamber's window. She wasn't moving.

He fell to his knees. His hands rested on his legs. He tried to control his breathing. The last time he felt like this, he'd just found out his parents passed.

He's going to die for this.

He clenched his jaw tight and wiped away the wells of his eyes as he stalked to his car. He fired his car back up and sped up the ramp.

"Jasper Kane's house. Quickest route."

Jasper Kane staggered into his house.

Beaten and bloodied, he walked into his nearest bathroom, unmasked, and turned on the light. He looked in the mirror and rubbed his head; the shots he took from his ex-girlfriend hurt him pretty bad. She punched right through his mask, and he felt every one of them.

I won't be able to go to work. There's no way I'm hiding this. Lying to Joyce isn't worth it, when I can just tell her I'm taking a vacation.

He took a moment to wash the dried blood off his face, then grabbed a towel and wiped his features dry. He was careful not to press too hard. His face was tender to the touch. He walked out into the living room and squirmed out of his jacket, dropping it on the floor.

"I knew you'd come sooner or later."

He looked up. It was The Sound.

"I don't have much left. Your partner kind of beat me up," Jasper told him. "You were right; she's a lot tougher than I ever imagined."

The Sound nodded yes. "You killed her … and now, you're going to pay for it."

"Wait-"

The Sound pelted him with punches. Some landed clean, some didn't. Jasper fell against a closet door, trapping himself in a corner. The Sound flung him to the ground and mounted him, pulling him up by his shirt. He gritted his teeth.

"I'm someone you took from. You took her from me!"

He punched him. Jasper's body limply hit the ground. He pulled him up again.

"You want to know who I *really* am?!"

Markus grabbed the top of his own mask and pulled up. The edges snapped free, moving past his neck, chin, and eyes. His face filled with bitterness, his eyes, filled with fury. His teeth clenched again. He dropped his mask by his side and grabbed another fistful of Jasper's shirt.

"You killed Vanessa! And for what?!"

Before Jasper could answer, Markus punched him again. This time, he let him go. Jasper barely moved.

"Vanessa?" Jasper whispered.

"Don't say her name!"

Markus gripped Jasper's throat and squeezed. His body writhed around, but not enough to move out of the Markus's grasp. "You've done this to so many people … how does it feel?" Markus asked. "How does it feel?!" he wailed.

"I left her … alive!" Jasper barely got out. "I … swear!"

Markus's grip loosened. "Who else was in that house?"

"Daphne … De La Rosa."

Markus loosened his grip more. Jasper smacked Markus's hands off his throat and immediately started a violent coughing fit so hard, a sharp pain settled in his side. When the coughing subsided, he stared at the ceiling. His eyes rolled to the side and landed on his counterpart slowly pacing, hands at his waist.

"She's dead? Vanessa's dead?" Jasper asked sheepishly.

"She's dead," Markus repeated.

"How do you know?" Jasper asked.

Markus continued pacing.

"Because I watched her stop breathing. That's how I know. Knife stuck inside her and bleeding everywhere."

"That's not my thing. You know that," Jasper said, followed by a cough.

"It's a bad time to argue semantics," Markus said.

"Agreed, but it's relevant information," Jasper countered. "I've never stabbed anyone. Never needed to. If that were my modus operandi, I would've stabbed you on the rooftop."

Markus didn't respond. Jasper's mind raced back and forth.

I care about her. I don't know why I left her, knowing what De La Rosa wanted to do. I should've backed down, not let her pursue me. Her blood is on my hands.

Jasper inched up to a sitting position against a wall.

"I can help you. We can find her."

Markus stopped pacing. "I almost killed you."

Jasper cleared his throat. "And I almost killed you. Call us even."

"I can't," Markus said. "We're not on the same side of this. You may have gotten to De La Rosa before, but she'll be more careful this time around - a little harder to get to. And it's not lost on me that if you catch her, you'll kill her."

Jasper winked. "Bingo."

23

The night turned into morning.

Jasper found himself at Markus's house. He had nowhere to go - Emma Starks gave him up to protect her brother, Patrick. Along with that, the woman he'd spent so much time with, the woman he envisioned making a life with, was dead. The loneliness was a familiar feeling for him, but he never thought he'd go back to it so fast.

It was devastating.

So he clung to Markus, the only constant in his life. He used the mutual interest in Vanessa as a way to sink his hooks in. As much as he wanted revenge on De La Rosa, he needed to bide his time. He also needed to feel safe doing so.

"TV: On."

Markus's command switched the TV on. "Local news." The channel switched. Jasper turned his head to the noise.

Daphne De La Rosa stood at the podium. Her bandaged hands clung to the small, wooden structure. She nodded at the press gathered in front of her. When the camera zoomed in, Markus noticed all the cuts on her face, as well as her swollen eye. It was different shades of purple, the kind of damage one assumes comes with a loss of eyesight. It was then that Markus realized it was Jasper that had done all the damage.

Lots of recorders stretched out, ready for her to speak. She cocked her head forward, her lips close to the microphone.

"Thank you all for coming on such short notice," Daphne said. "There's one thing I wanna make clear before I start: My hand's been forced. I take no pleasure in this announcement."

Daphne's eyes led to the podium's angled surface.

"I had a run-in with the Ivory Fox, as she's called in the news. As you can see, she attacked me ferociously, and without provocation. After being warned several times to stop, I had no other choice but to use lethal force as a means to subdue her."

Another officer patted her on the shoulder. She looked his way and nodded, then returned her gaze forward.

"I'm also at liberty to tell the public, that I sought and received permission from the higher-ups to head a Task Force that will rid the streets of these masked menaces. So that the people can return to their daily lives, we will move as quickly as possible."

"What does that mean?" an impatient reporter blurted out.

"It means…" she looked up from her paper and down at the reporter. "It means that tonight, when the sun goes down, we ask that all civilians be off the street, until sun-up tomorrow. If you're not, it'll be assumed that you are aiding criminals. During that 12-hour period, there will be a standing invitation for the masked to turn themselves in peacefully. Just call us, and we'll come pick you up. The last thing we need is for someone to be misidentified, walking to the police station."

A reporter said, "What if these masks don't? I can see lots of these people just staying in and waiting it out."

Daphne smirked and said, "We have our suspicions and leads. We also have ones we're sure about, ones we've picked up before. It's not as tough as you're making it sound." Her eyes left the reporter and looked directly into the camera. "Our main goal is to return the power to the city. For too long, it's been overrun by people thinking they can do our jobs without working within the rules of the law. We will make this city safer for you, your children, and your children's children."

Her eyes burned with intensity when she said, "And I will *personally* make sure The Sound and the Broken Skull are brought to justice. You have my word. God bless."

She walked away from the podium, a slather of questions following as she walked with other officers back into the police station.

"TV: Off."

The TV shut off.

"I refuse to turn myself in," Jasper said to Markus. "Out of the question. I'm sure I could just leave town. There would be no harm. I don't trust that she's going to just pick these people up, book them, and have them sit in jail for … whatever amount of time they irrationally determine."

Markus had a faraway look in his eyes. Jasper noticed.

"You're contemplating this?" Jasper asked.

"Maybe Vanessa being killed was a sign," Markus said. He stood up from the couch. "She didn't really ask for the life she got. She witnessed her parents' murder. I'm sure if she had a choice, she would've been content just being my personal assistant. She has no business being talked about in the past tense, and it's because of us. My conscience will be clear if I turn myself in. So will yours."

Memories came flooding back to Jasper. He remembered when he first met her, and how nice she was. Even when she found out he was the Broken Skull, she was somewhat forgiving. Someone normal would have turned their back on him without a second thought. She wanted to be patient with him. He wouldn't let her.

"I can't do it, and I stand by my assertion that she'll do more to the ones captured than she's letting on. I don't trust it, nor should you."

"When the sun goes down, I'm going to do what's right - keep the ones around me safe. That's what Vanessa would want," Markus said. "I know you have it in you to make the right decision."

"I do, and I will."

Turn the Page …

Survive the Night: Part II

Haven't heard from you in like forever. Are you okay?

Yeah, I'm ok. How are you holding up?

Not so good. I caught that detective on TV talking about you...

I'll be ok.

What will you do? Turn yourself in? Leave the state?????

I still have 15 minutes.

I'm worried. I'd like to come visit before the sun goes down.

No Mare. I don't want you in the middle of this mess.

So you're just going to sit at home and think?

Yes. That's the plan.

Are you afraid?

It doesn't pay to be afraid.

Cut the macho bull with me Markus.

My asst. is dead and people want to kill me. Not afraid. Angry.

Is there a way I can help?

I'll get in touch with you when this blows over.

I love you Markus. Stay safe.

I love you too.

Markus dropped his phone on the table.

"Time is running out," Jasper told Markus.

"I know," Markus snapped. "It's a decision that's not so easy to make, especially when other people's lives are at stake."

"You think I have no lives at stake?" Jasper snapped back. "I have a loved one in the hospital, and the other … I'm not quite sure."

"I imagine as long as they don't wear a mask, they'll be okay."

"So will you, or did you forget? The detective doesn't know who you are. Your nobility is admirable, but ultimately … foolish."

Nightfall approached. A siren blared, almost deafening. The two looked toward the front door. Markus looked through the back windows. He felt a small rumble right below his feet. He looked down. It was confirmed.

"Proximity check."

A hologram shot up in front of Markus. Jasper raised his eyebrows in surprise. He was more impressed than astounded. An outline of his house and the road leading to it popped up on a flat grid. He watched as multiple cars and trucks darted up the road. They were approaching as fast as the sun fell. He turned toward Jasper.

"What did you do? Who did you tell you were here?" he asked, his voice full of accusation.

Markus's words broke Jasper's concentration on the approaching vehicles. He looked at Markus. "I … I didn't …" he shook his head no at him. "Nobody knows I'm here."

"Are you sure nobody knows?" Markus asked him again, his voice raised. His heart pounded in anticipation of Jasper's answer.

"I'm sure," Jasper said, his voice raised, as well. His breathing started to labor. "I don't– …"

Markus placed his hand up.

"Let me think."

He kept his hand up, but dipped his head low and closed his eyes. His breathing slowed with every passing second. Markus tried his hardest to turn the situation into a positive, but he didn't see one.

The siren stopped. Markus opened his eyes. He knew what he needed to do.

"Markus Doubleday … come out with your hands up."

It sounded like a megaphone. It sounded like De La Rosa.

"If you don't come out, we will be forced to come in! You have until the count of three!"

It was quiet. The air was thick with tension. Jasper and Markus looked at each other, both afraid to exhale too loudly, both listening for anything that could tip them off about what was going on outside.

"One!"

"Markus?" Jasper said.

"Two!"

"How are we going to get out of here?" Jasper asked.

"Three!"

It got quiet again.

"How'd you–"

Gunfire rang out. Bullets came through the windows. Markus sprinted to the basement door.

"Through here!" he said.

Jasper grabbed his bag and followed right behind him. Markus placed his hand on the sensor right by the door. He heard it unlock. He opened the door and let Jasper through first, and then shut the door behind him. He heard the door lock again. He didn't know how long the door would last, if De La Rosa and whoever was with her decided they wanted to open it.

The platform brought the two down to the garage level. "We're a go!" Markus yelled. Jasper was confused with it all but stopped short when the whole room changed. Computers, cars and suits, everywhere.

"You still haven't answered my question," Jasper said.

"No more questions," Markus said.

His suit dropped. While he slid it on, he told Jasper, "Just because they seem to know our identities, it doesn't mean that others do." He slid his boots on and fastened them. "The door will buy us time, but we need to get out of here." He slid his gloves on and pulled on them hard, straightening and widening his fingers out until it felt snug. "We have a better chance braving it out there than we do sitting in my house."

"I agree." Jasper unzipped his bag and reached in it, pulling out his mask and trench coat, among other things. While he got dressed, he said, "I feel confident that we know the streets better than they do." He listened to the ongoing gunfire, but continued to dress, undeterred.

When they finished dressing, Markus walked towards his car. Jasper followed.

"I wasn't sure what we were taking," Jasper commented. "I assumed, but–"

"We're taking the one that's not normal," Markus said. "Let's go."

He heard a noise. Sounded like it came from the Recovery Room, behind him and Jasper. He looked at him. Jasper looked back. The two turned around.

"When are we leaving?"

It was Vanessa.

ABOUT THE AUTHOR

Derryan Derrough is the author of *The Sound You Made*. When he isn't writing, he enjoys coaching Wrestling, cooking, doing introvert things, and hanging out with his wife and kids. To keep up with him, you can follow him on Twitter at @derryanderrough.